Instinctively, Allie froze.

With one hand still on the doorknob, she stood in the doorway. Blushing wasn't her style, but then again, staring at a half-naked stranger draped only in a towel wasn't an everyday occurrence. She noted the firm lines of the man's broad chest. His legs weren't half bad, either.

"Hi," she said brightly, doing her best not to take a more leisurely look.

At least ten seconds passed.

"Hello."

A rivulet at the base of his throat streamed downward into the dark mat of chest hair. Crystal droplets beaded the dark hair on his head. He smelled soapy clean.

"Nice meeting you," she said. "Whoever you are."

Dear Reader,

Welcome to the Silhouette **Special Edition** experience! With your search for consistently satisfying reading in mind, every month the authors and editors of Silhouette **Special Edition** aim to offer you a stimulating blend of deep emotions and high romance.

The name Silhouette **Special Edition** and the distinctive arch on the cover represent a commitment—a commitment to bring you six sensitive, substantial novels each month. In the pages of a Silhouette **Special Edition**, compelling true-to-life characters face riveting emotional issues—and come out winners. All the authors in the series strive for depth, vividness and warmth in writing these stories of living and loving in today's world.

The result, we hope, is romance you can believe in. Deeply emotional, richly romantic, infinitely rewarding—that's the Silhouette **Special Edition** experience. Come share it with us—six times a month!

From all the authors and editors of Silhouette **Special Edition**,

Best wishes,

Leslie Kazanjian,
Senior Editor

JENNIFER MIKELS

Freedom's Just Another Word

Silhouette Special Edition

Published by Silhouette Books New York

America's Publisher of Contemporary Romance

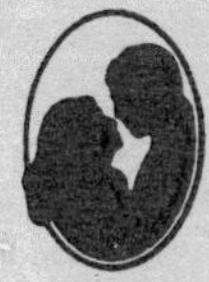

SILHOUETTE BOOKS
300 East 42nd St., New York, N.Y. 10017

ISBN: 0-373-09623-2

First Silhouette Books printing September 1990

Printed in the U.S.A.

Books by Jennifer Mikels

Silhouette Special Edition

A Sporting Affair #66
Whirlwind #124
Remember the Daffodils # 478
Double Identity #521
Stargazer #574
Freedom's Just Another Word #623

Silhouette Romance

Lady of the West #462
Maverick #487
Perfect Partners #511
The Bewitching Hour #551

JENNIFER MIKELS

started out an avid fan of historical novels, which eventually led her to contemporary romances, which in turn led her to try her hand at penning her own novel. She quickly found she preferred romance fiction with its happy endings to the technical writing she'd done for a public-relations firm. Between writing and raising two teenage boys, the Phoenix-based author has little time left for hobbies, though she does enjoy cross-country skiing and antique shopping with her husband.

"Anywhere you hang your heart is home."
—Allie Gentry
MONTANA
IDAHO
CALIFORNIA
OKLAHOMA
TEXAS
ILLINOIS
NEW YORK
VERMONT
MASSACHUSETTS

Prologue

Black Walls? Joshua MacKenzie reminded himself to make do. Be grateful for a place to stay. Be flexible. He knew during the past few years that housing had become a problem around the college. When he'd accepted the position as a history professor at Wainwright College, he'd told himself that he would overlook a few inconveniences to be near friends like Nate Henderson, to be back in Vermont again.

Standing beside him, Nate shifted his stance while Josh viewed the apartment that his colleague had secured for him. At the touch of Nate's hand on his shoulder, Josh assumed that Nate, being twenty years older than his thirty-one, was satisfying some paternal streak. "Edith and I will come over later and help you paint if you want to change anything."

Josh eyed the narrow kitchen that he could cross in two strides. "I'll be fine," he said, staring at the network of lines beneath Nate's eyes.

"I'm glad. As I told you earlier during dinner, we'd had another apartment tentatively leased. But," he added conspiratorially low, "Dean Forsythe took so long in making a decision about his choice to fill the history vacancy that we couldn't retain the other apartment for you."

Josh repeated the lie. "This is—this is just fine." The apartment was small: one bedroom with a single bed and a small dresser. Adjacent to the kitchen was a large room with black walls and clean but worn furniture. The sagging cushions of the moss-green sofa promised discomfort. Scanning the three windows that looked out on the street, Josh noted that he'd adopted nearly a dozen wilting plants. The house was vintage nineteenth century with narrow clapboard siding, stained yellow; high ceilings; tall, symmetrically placed windows and a mansard roof. Renovated somewhat, it was termed a "tenement" house a century ago simply because the upper floor of the box-like building was used by renters. Downstairs were the quaint quarters of the Vanovitches, with their rooms full of antiques. The upstairs, divided in half, offered Josh and his neighbor the privacy of their own kitchens and bedrooms at opposite ends of a short hall.

"We're glad you were offered the tenure. I've missed you," Nate added then turned away as if embarrassed. "What do you suppose possessed someone to paint the walls this color?"

Josh smiled, sensing his colleague hoped that he hadn't lost his sense of humor. "A morose personality?" He decided that he could endure sharing a bathroom with his neighbor, and he did like the plank floors and the bay window. And a French door opened onto a small terrace where he could sit outside and grade papers during the afternoon.

"Actually," Nate informed him, "the previous occupant was an artist and obviously—ah—ah—"

Josh led the way toward the door. "Eccentric."

Following him into the hallway, Nate mumbled, "Seems likely." While they descended the steep flight of stairs inside the building to retrieve Josh's luggage from the car, he did his best to ease the older man's concern. After he was settled in and developed some routine with his classes, he would look for another apartment. For now, this one would do.

Allison Gentry peered out the window of her car and watched the man juggling four suitcases and a garment bag from his car toward the door at the side of the building. The new neighbor, Allison deducted.

Beneath the moonlight, she could only gather impressions. He was tall and obviously young, judging by the broad shoulders and the straightness of his back before his body bent over from the burden of his luggage.

Allison fiddled with the car radio dial until she heard Neil Compson's smooth voice. "Stay tuned to KFKQ, Vermont's favorite soft rock station. This is Neil Compson at eight-thirty on a clear, brisk autumn night. For the next half hour settle back to more of this week's top forty. At nine, KFKQ brings you the husky soft sound of Allie Gentry and night music for lovers."

Allie smiled, zipped her yellow Mustang out into the street and began humming along with Sheena Easton.

Chapter One

It was still dark outside the bedroom window as Josh crawled out of bed.

He padded into the dismal adjacent room. With its nocturnal paint job, it would remain shadowed in darkness throughout the day. On a frown, he snatched up his bathrobe while eyeing the air conditioner in the kitchen window of the L-shaped room. In summer, the air conditioner probably rumbled. And no doubt, the steam radiator hissed during the winter.

His shaving gear in hand, he shuffled into the hallway. The spicy aroma of something that resembled spaghetti sauce greeted him. No one cooked spaghetti at five in the morning. On a yawn, he flung open the door to the bathroom that he shared with someone named Al Gentry. In fifteen minutes, after a shave and a shower, he'd be less muddled. Then, maybe, even his dreary apartment wouldn't look so bad.

Allison finished undressing and slid on a bathrobe before hurrying into the kitchen to check the sauce simmering on the stove. Turning the burner lower, she calculated that she would have half an hour for a relaxing bath before the spaghetti sauce was done. She'd eat dinner and then go to bed. The night at the radio station hadn't been easy. She sympathized with Ray Clements, the station manager. Ever since new ownership a month ago, Clements had been caught in a format conflict. The new owner, B.J. Vannen, needed to make a decision. At present, he'd made only one. He'd placed his son, Bill Vannen Jr., in charge of programming. Junior knew nothing about management and even less about programming, she decided as she reached forward and opened the bathroom door.

Instinctively she froze. With one hand still on the doorknob, she stood in the doorway. Blushing wasn't her style, but then staring at half-naked strangers draped only in a towel wasn't an everyday occurrence. She noted the firm lines of his broad chest. Unlike the regulars at the local spa who pumped iron, he didn't have muscles that looked like baseballs stuffed beneath the skin. The flesh was smooth, flowing but muscular. His legs weren't half bad, either. "Hi," she said brightly, while doing her best not to take a more leisurely look.

At least ten silent seconds passed.

Standing at the sink, a razor threateningly close to the artery in his neck, Josh couldn't think of anything more intelligent than, "Hello."

A rivulet at the base of his throat streamed downward into the dark mat of chest hair. Crystal droplets beaded the dark hair on his head. He smelled soapy clean. "Nice meeting you," she said, noting not only that he wore a puzzled expression but also that he hadn't snatched on his bathrobe. "Whoever you are."

He turned off the faucet. "Who are you?"

"Your neighbor."

He shook his head. "No."

At his confused look, she smiled. "Yes."

"But, Al—"

"That's me," she announced. "You just moved in last night, didn't you?" To her relief, he set the straight razor down on the sink.

"Yes." He continued to frown.

In all honesty, she had to admit that even frowning he was better than average looking. Incredibly better.

"The mailbox says Al," he told her.

"Oh, Mrs. Vanovitch ran out of space on the nameplate." She offered a hand. "Allison Gentry. Allie. You'll probably be— What is your name?"

"Joshua. Joshua MacKenzie."

"On the mailbox panel, you'll be JoshMack."

"Mack?"

Allison set her palm against the doorjamb. "Or JMackenz. Mrs. Vanovitch has space for only eight letters. So you'll be abbreviated."

"Mackenz?"

"Uh, huh."

He looked confused.

He also looked like a perfect specimen, Allie mused. Shampooed, his dark brown hair cut neatly—perfectly—wasn't messed. He stood a good six inches taller than she did. Nicely shaped dark brows, deep-set brown eyes, an aristocratic nose and well-defined lips presented a perfect face on a perfect body. The last thing Allie wanted was another perfect person in her life. "You're not done in here, yet, are you?"

As if trying to remember, he ran his finger along the smooth side of his face and looked in the mirror at his half-lathered jaw. "No, I'm not."

"Okay. I'll give you five."

"No!"

Allie swung a look back as he finished knotting the tie on a white terrycloth robe. "No?"

"I meant wait," he insisted. "We have a problem."

"What problem?" Allison stared at his serious expression and felt herself fighting another smile.

"It's five in the morning. I need to use the bathroom before I leave for work. I have a precise schedule."

She tipped her head. "Precise?"

"Extremely. What time do you need to leave for work?"

His demanding tone should have annoyed her. But she sensed that when he asked a question he expected an answer. "Eight-thirty," she answered.

"Does it take you three hours to get ready?"

"I haven't been to bed yet."

Confusion clouded his eyes again.

On an inhale, Allie drew in the woodsy scent of his shaving cream. "I leave for work at eight-thirty at night." When he didn't respond, she went on, "I just got home. You see, I like to come home and start my dinner—"

Josh took a guess. "Spaghetti?"

"Yes, tonight, I'm having spaghetti."

"To you, it may be night, but to the rest of Vermont it's morning."

"Yes, but we're discussing me, not everyone. So," she went on, "I come home and take a nice leisurely bath for about half an hour. It helps me unwind."

"I have to ask. From doing *what*?"

"I'm a deejay at night at KFKQ."

He braced a hand on the doorjamb as if holding it up. "I've never met a deejay before."

"I didn't say that I was an alien. I'm a deejay." She closed one eye and peered at him. "What do you do?"

"I'm a professor at the college."

"Ah, one of those academia types who doesn't know that dogcatchers and garbagemen and deejays also inhabit the world?"

"I'm not a snob," he said defensively.

"Just oblivious."

He pushed away from the door. "Just a minute."

"Don't have a fit. I'm only clarifying the differences between us, which is good. It will make sharing this bathroom easier for us."

"More difficult, I would say."

"Not really." She sniffed. "I have to stir my spaghetti sauce. You'd better come along," she said while strolling away from him. "We need to work out a schedule, or we'll be running into a problem tomorrow morning, too."

Josh hesitated, then dabbing the towel at his face, he followed her down the hall. "I can only take a few minutes."

"How long? Precisely." She heard his short laugh and decided a sense of humor lurked close to the surface.

"I think that you're right," he said with such seriousness that Allie couldn't help grinning again. "We do need a schedule."

"Of course we do." She led the way into her kitchen and hurried to the stove. Without a glance back to see if he'd followed, she began stirring the sauce. "Otherwise, we'll be opening that door on each other all the time."

Stacks of papers were strewn on the kitchen floor. While Josh stepped over them to reach her, she lifted the wooden spoon and offered him a taste of the sauce. "How's this taste?"

Cautiously he sampled the sauce. It was pungent and heavily laced with garlic. "Good."

She gave him a quick, pleased smile. "So now, about that schedule."

He pushed back the cuff of his robe and squinted at his watch.

Farsighted, Allie deducted, setting the spoon back in the pot. "Time is important to you in the morning."

He sighed with relief that she comprehended what he considered a problem.

Facing him, she grabbed his wrist and turned his arm so she could see his watch. "Good. It's only five twenty-five. You still have a few minutes."

"Uh—" Josh glanced at his wristwatch then at hers. "Why didn't you look at your own?"

"I wanted to make sure we were synchronized."

He doubted they ever would be.

"Since you have a few minutes—" she started, turning away and heading out of her apartment.

Josh trailed behind her. "I really don't—"

"Not even one minute?" she asked with a glance back, holding up a finger. "I need someone to help haul something to my apartment from the storage room."

"Where's the storage room?"

"At the corner of the hall."

A frown passed swiftly over his face. "All right," he answered and wondered why he'd bothered. She was already halfway down the hall.

"Emile Lafitte, the previous tenant in your apartment, promised to help me, but that was the same day he disappeared during the night."

Josh fell in step beside her. "Disappeared where?"

"No foul play. He left without paying the rent." She grinned impishly up at him.

A blond bundle of energy, he decided. He felt an openness, a friendliness that usually took people weeks, sometimes months, to offer others. "What did he—Emile—do for a living?"

"He was an artist. Why?"

"Black walls. Mirrored ceilings."

She giggled. "The apartment is awful, isn't it? Emile had some odd ideas about decorating." Her tone turned matter-of-fact. "But then he was an odd man."

"In what way?"

She noted the amusement in his eyes. "He was positive that he was once Toulouse-Lautrec. And like the French painter, he seemed to have a similar inclination for certain types of ladies."

Josh swung a look at her.

"Ladies of the evening. Be grateful. He could have done the room in the painter's favorite colors—orange and green." She flung open a door.

Dark and musty, it appeared the gathering place for the discards of every tenant who'd ever occupied the house. As she wound her way around an antiquated sewing machine, Josh remained firmly rooted in the doorway. "What do you want moved?"

"One suitcase."

Her request seemed simple enough. Head bent, he sidestepped a broken rocking horse. "Are you moving?"

Abruptly she halted to look back at him. "Moving?"

Josh braked a hairbreadth from her. He smelled the scent of lavender and felt himself leaning closer, wondering where she'd dabbed the summer fragrance. Somewhere outside, a car horn blared. The world was waking up. He felt as if he was being lulled to some dark, enchanting place as he stared at her eyes. A practical man, he'd never believed in body chemistry. But the scent she wore was alluring. And scientific proof had been offered that an attraction often began because of a propensity for another person's scent. He nearly laughed. What a dumb thing to think about while staring at a beautiful woman. And damn, but she was beautiful.

"Why did you ask if I was moving?"

By her tone, he guessed that she'd repeated her question. "The suitcase?" he said in a questioning voice.

"Oh, no, I'm not moving."

"But the suitcase—"

"I have some old records stored in it."

"Bank receipts?" He heard her soft giggle.

"45 RPMs." With her hand, she gestured toward the floor. "It's sort of—"

"A trunk," he finished for her. He wasn't out of shape. He didn't believe in a person getting soft mentally or physically. But a muscle in his arm quivered protestingly as he lifted the trunk. She had bricks in it, he decided. Josh grabbed an edge of it and repositioned it on his back.

An eternity seemed to pass before he deposited the trunk inside her apartment. Winded, he collapsed on it, wondering if he could have a heart attack at his age. He felt the pulse in his wrist. It was hammering away.

"You don't look out of shape."

He scowled up at her. "For a living, I carry books, not furniture," he managed between deep breaths and stared down at the floor again while he drew a long, lung-filling breath.

He sat as if frozen. She'd teased him before, for he looked strong enough to be a furniture mover. At his continued silence, she stepped closer, noting his eyes were riveted to a tapestry-patterned diaper bag. "Is something wrong?"

He jabbed a finger at the bag. "That? Do you have a baby?" Not waiting for her response, he glanced around her apartment as if he expected to be assaulted. "This isn't going to work out. I need my sleep. I have to get up early. I have to get up at—"

The man was definitely the stressful type. She'd lived with a family just like that. The slightest unexpected change was treated as catastrophic. "No baby," she assured him, turning away. "The bag holds my cosmetics." A lithograph of the Rhine, a Christmas present from her sister Sarah, hung on a wall crookedly. With a fingertip, Allie nudged the frame to straighten it. "Sensibly, all diaper bags are plastic-lined. I move around a lot. If something spills, then I just wipe up the inside of the bag. Makes sense, doesn't it?"

At the moment, she could have told him that the world was flat and he would have believed her. Hadn't a confirmed coffee drinker who rarely ate anything before nine in the morning just eaten a sampling of spaghetti sauce for breakfast?

"People use suitcases for everything. But they're really impractical."

As she pointed, he looked at the gym bag.

"It holds my shoes. Soles are dirty. Why put them in the same bag with clean clothes? Right?"

Too intent on breathing normally again, he simply nodded agreeably.

"Listen, I've been thinking."

"This could be disastrous," he mumbled.

"Did you say something?" she asked while taking down the lithograph.

Josh decided the bare wall looked better. The apartment was sparsely furnished with obvious thrift-store treasures: a soft, cushiony parpazan chair, a grotesque-looking floor lamp and a scratched table with an Oriental lamp. Rounding out the careless motif were several painted crates. The lithograph was expensive and out-of-place.

"You're not my type obviously."

He caught himself frowning instead of agreeing. "I'm not?" She gave him a spine-tingling smile. Weaker men probably groveled for it. He was of a more disciplined nature, he reminded himself while he ignored a quick tightening in his stomach.

"No offense. But you're too—too—well, you did say that you're a professor, didn't you?"

"Yes."

"Of what?"

"History."

She grinned. "See that proves my point."

Josh strained to follow her thinking.

"If you had a time machine, where would you go?"

"A time machine?"

"À la H.G. Wells," she said with a wave of her hand.

"I'd travel to—"

"The past?"

"Of course," he answered without hesitation.

"See? I'd go to the future. I'd want to know all the things that might happen after I've left or at least those that happened before I'm here again."

"Here again?"

"You don't believe in reincarnation, either?"

"Never gave it much thought."

"I thought not." She opened the trunk. "Well, do you see my point?"

"Not exactly."

"I don't care what happens in the past."

Was he really having such a conversation before six in the morning?

"Ergo. If you wanted to go back all the time and I wanted to go forward, we'd never be together. So what's really important is that we can work this out."

"By this, do you mean our sharing the bathroom?"

She did an about-face. "I love this song," she said, holding up a record. "Spike Jones. Silly but different. I can't play it at the station." She wrinkled her nose. "I did when I worked at the Boston station." Mischief sprang into her eyes. "We were playing mostly music to call the paramedics by. That record caused quite an uproar." She flung her hands out in a hopeless gesture. "People demand predictableness, don't they?"

"It's reassuring."

"Stale," she countered.

At the certainty in her voice, he nearly smiled again.

"Now, about the bathroom. Women need more time. We primp, you know."

"I've heard that."

"I'm practical, by nature. I see no real problem. You're gone all day, right?"

"Yes."

"So except for when I come home from work, and you're getting ready for work, we'll probably never see each other."

Josh nodded, wondering why the idea suddenly seemed depressing.

"Are you left- or right-handed?"

"Right."

She beamed. "That's great. I'm left."

"And that's great?"

"Not always. The world is made for right-handed people."

"No, I meant that you're left-handed and I'm right-handed. That's great?" he asked, wondering why someone who prided himself in being intellectual was having difficulty following her conversation.

"Oh, yes," she said, turning and strolling toward the door of her apartment. "Now being a lefty, I've learned to be flexible."

I'm not, Josh nearly said as he followed her to the door. He kept quiet, guessing that she'd already made that assumption about him.

"So I'll put all of my things, like my rainbow gel pump, on the left side of the sink. And you can put all of your things on the right side. Of course, if you need to borrow my toothpaste, you can but—"

"I use baking soda."

She made a face. "I see."

"No, I don't think you do. Compatibility is very important."

"Yes, for lovers," she said. "But you see my point? We aren't compatible. So that means we won't have any carnal urges complicating everything if we happen to pass each other in the middle of the night in the hallway. And I may not be at KFKQ long. When I accepted the position at the radio station and left Oklahoma to take over the graveyard shift, I really didn't like the idea. I'm a morning person usually. So this might be only a temporary adjustment for you. And the way I calculate everything—"

Josh took a deep breath and prepared himself.

"You'll be leaving for work when I get home."

His frown deepened. "Not exactly."

"As I said, I get home at four-thirty in the morning and take a bath to unwind before going to bed," she repeated on a sigh as if he were slow-witted.

"But I get up at five to take a shower before going to work."

"Yes, we've established that."

"But we haven't solved our problem," he reminded her as he stepped into the hallway.

"Except for a half hour in the morning, I won't bother you."

Josh could have told her differently. He wasn't immune to good-looking women, especially a Goldie Hawn look-alike with enormous blue eyes and curves in all the right places.

Her idea was ludicrous. She already bothered him.

With her quick turn away, her wheat-colored hair swung and lightly brushed his jaw. "I'll try to stall an extra fifteen minutes. By then, you should be done. And if we should pass each other, then pretend I'm your sister. You'd better hurry or you'll be late," she added and smiled again before she closed her apartment door.

He frowned, feeling as if the hallway was suddenly a shade darker. Who was she kidding? She charged a room with her energy. What male could ignore such a jolt? Sister? That was the most ludicrous idea of all.

Chapter Two

"Are you settled in?" Nate questioned, joining Josh in the cafeteria lunch line.

Josh eyed the meat loaf and chose a salad. He still had to go grocery shopping. "Semi settled." He grinned as he thought about Allison Gentry.

Nate nudged his arm. "Don't buy the Waldorf salad." He shook his gray head and set the salad plate back on the counter. "The apples are questionable sometimes."

Josh grabbed a tossed salad instead. "I have a neighbor. A lovely neighbor."

"Excuse me."

At the male voice behind them, both men stepped aside.

"I forgot a spoon," Dean Forsythe offered. He was a tall, rigid-looking, gray-haired man with dark bags under his eyes like a raccoon's mask.

"See that," Nate gibed low as the Dean turned away. "The higher echelon of Wainwright isn't perfect."

Josh responded with a quick smile.

"So back to your neighbor. What's the problem?"

While they searched for a table, Josh went on, "She's a charming blonde. She talks nonstop. Her clock is backward. She works nights and eats spaghetti for breakfast."

"Sounds interesting."

"Not dull," Josh admitted.

"That's good." Nate touched his shoulder as they settled at a table. "Stodgy has been known to fit Wainwright. With all the older-than-Moses types here, you might find that peculiar woman will keep you from feeling as if you're a museum piece."

Smiling, Josh glanced around him. The mood in the cafeteria wasn't any different at Wainwright than at other colleges. The noise was deafening with chatter and laughter. But Josh felt the sedateness surrounding him whenever he strolled into the faculty lounge.

"Feel on display?" Nate asked.

Other than a few of the female students who had a thing for professors, few students paid attention to him. But the faculty had found a new topic of interest, he realized. "Is there spinach between my teeth?" he asked, baring a toothy smile for Nate.

"No, you look fairly close to perfect." Nate smiled. "Some of those stares are envious ones for your youth and position. The remainder of our faculty are probably rifling daggers at you. You're the youngest tenured professor here. You do know that you and two other professors are in contention for the chair of the history department?"

Josh nodded. "I came here hoping that I would be."

"I'd vote for you if I had a say in it. However, you have one roadblock."

"I'm too young."

"Ah, yes. Small, private institutions, especially those that began in the last century, are known for archaic thinking," he reminded Josh. "So you realize that you represent a less responsible age group."

"I'm thirty-one, not fifteen."

"The average professor here is fifty-two. You're a baby, my boy."

Josh grinned.

"They'll be watching you to see if you fit the mold."

Fitting in was something he'd tried to do all his life. "I will. Within reason," he added, then laughed. "I'm not relinquishing my Tina Turner albums just for their sake."

"I'm so glad that you haven't changed. There's a tendency among the faculty here to let social atrophy set in. The history department needs a chairman who'll fit the mold on occasion but not become stagnant. People with young ideas are what Wainwright needs." He chuckled. "A good scandal might help."

At three o'clock, Allie hustled herself out of bed. After an hour in the basement laundry room, she went over her playing schedule for the evening. Though not a creature of habit, she disciplined herself with certain routines. The morning bath, a definite bedtime and a firm hour set aside to schedule her airtime that evening. Though she'd been with KFKQ only three months, she had a decent nighttime following because she'd geared the late segment of her program, mostly after eleven, with music for lovers.

At her previous job she was with a country and western station. Before that, she'd worked at a classical music station in Boston. But sonnets by Elizabeth Barrett Browning sprinkled between concertos wouldn't do at KFKQ. Sitting on the kitchen floor, she fanned pages of her personal log.

An old building, the house held no secrets. She heard her new neighbor's footsteps as he climbed the stairs. Weary footsteps. Nothing harder than the first day on a new job, even a familiar job.

Josh's first reaction was surprise and then pleasure. He stood outside his apartment door and stared down at the covered casserole outside the door. Even without bending forward, he could read the note attached to it: Made too much. Your favorite neighbor.

A laugh slipped out. He was amazed to hear it. He'd thought nothing or anyone would spark his laughter this evening. He should have known better, he realized with a glance down the hall.

When he'd parked the car, he'd planned to make a quick sandwich, take a hot shower and then climb into a soft bed. He definitely hadn't wanted to hear another voice. Now, one particular husky, feminine one seemed to be beckoning to him.

He opened the door, set the casserole in the refrigerator, and with the grocery bag cradled in his arm, he strolled down the hallway.

"Just being neighborly," he said as Allie opened the door. He looked into the bag that he cradled in one arm. "I have corn beef, Swiss cheese and rye bread from Mr. Myer's delicatessen. A bottle of wine from Tony's Italian restaurant across from the college," he went on. "And apple fritters from Mrs. Schultz's bakery."

Allie laughed. "I see that you've already had the tour of the town."

"I taught here several years ago on a temporary basis while one of the professors was on sabbatical. But teachers I'd never met before felt compelled to take me for walks during each break I had."

"And introduce you to Barrington's culinary attractions?"

"Yes. But then, what else is there?"

She opened the door wider. "Come in. Barrington is known for three things—its nearby skiing, a smorgasbord of ethnic delis and restaurants, and of course, Wainwright."

Josh followed her into the kitchen.

"You said that you taught here before?"

"I was offered tenure this time. That's why I came back."

"Then you knew that Wainwright was so—?" She paused, unsure if he would take offense at her opinion of the college.

"Proper?"

She smiled over her shoulder at him. "Yes," she answered, deciding his word was better than priggish. "Teaching minds and morals is the code there."

"You sound disapproving."

"Stuffy best describes the faculty."

"We're not that bad."

"Not you, maybe."

He cocked a brow. "Maybe?"

She laughed. "No, I guess, you aren't. Anyone who uses a Snoopy glass to hold his toothbrush can't be all bad."

He set the bag on a kitchen counter. As he straightened beside her, he caught a whiff of lavender again. "Thanks for the spaghetti. I'll heat it tomorrow night. But since I have all this," he said, touching the top of the grocery bag, "can I entice you?"

"That's a loaded question, Professor."

He grinned. "To have—" He paused and glanced at his watch. "Is this your breakfast or dinner?"

"Breakfast. Do you have pickles?"

"That's important?"

"Vital."

"I have pickles."

The woman smiled more than anyone he'd ever met, Josh realized. She pulled sunshine into a room. He wondered if she could do that in the dark abyss that he called his living room.

"I love picnics."

"Picnics?" At the sweep of her arm, he scanned the room. When he'd entered it that morning, he'd noticed a messiness and thought that was what bothered him about the room. But he'd been too preoccupied with the problem at hand—namely her—to notice much about her apartment. Slowly he scanned his surroundings now. Pots of phony geraniums were set in helter-skelter fashion on the floor. In one corner was a phony pine tree.

"I don't have a kitchen table."

"Should I ask?"

"Ask what?" She handed him two glasses. One was a crystal goblet. The other looked like a mason jar.

"Why you don't have one?"

"I move too much to invest in furniture. When I moved in, Mrs. Vanovitch promised a new table, but she seems to always forget."

He heard an impishness in her voice that matched the sparkle of amusement in her eyes. But his thoughts focused more on the warmth of her breath near his face.

"We could sit on the terrace if you like brisk fresh air."

"Lead. I'll follow." She wore jeans so tight that she looked poured into them and a yellow sweatshirt that was so baggy no curves were distinguishable.

"You sit here." She indicated one of the wrought iron chairs. "The view is nicer. Unless you like to look at garbage cans. I've never understood why they were always painted gray or yucky green. Why aren't they painted a brighter color?"

"For what purpose?"

His question didn't surprise her. She'd guessed that he would insist on everything having a purpose or reason. "One summer when my family was vacationing at a house on the ocean, I wanted to collect seashells," she said while setting the food on the table. "My mother asked the same question."

"And what did you say?"

"I didn't. Being a child, I was soundly intimidated by her stern frown. But now I could say that I like to watch sunrises and enjoy reading trashy spy thrillers for no real reason."

"Except they please you."

She met the smile in his eyes. He would be easy to like, but she didn't want him to be too appealing, she reminded herself. "Astute, Professor. Yes, that's my reason. Odd, isn't it, that collectively my family has dozens of degrees and no one has ever figured that out?"

Josh stared down at her scruffy-looking sneakers. She was a freethinker. In the classroom, he considered them the cream of the crop. In his personal life, he avoided them. They rebelled against everything he considered sacred. He was a traditional man. He'd worked hard and long for simple things: home, family and friends.

"Why did you come back to Wainwright?"

He gave up his preoccupation with the untied laces that hung like useless threads from her shoes. "I wanted to do more than teach."

Chomping down on a pickle, she tipped her head questioningly.

"The chairman of the history department is retiring. I decided to see if I could get appointed to the position."

She arched a brow. "As department chairman?"

"No one has been named yet to take over for him."

"And you think that you have a chance even though you're the newest professor at the college?"

"I think so."

"You must have an impressive résumé."

"Better than decent. And several of the professors are close to retirement age. That gives me a little edge. The Board of Regents might want to place someone in the position who'll stay."

"And you'd want to stay?"

"Of course."

"For decades?"

He grinned at the disdainful tone of her voice. "If possible."

She grimaced. "I couldn't imagine doing that. In broadcasting, no one expects a lifetime job. Managerial positions provide security, but deejays are the gypsies of broadcasting. There's a bullet set aside for anyone whose voice comes over the airwaves. The public is fickle. They tire of listening to the same voice every day. I guess the same problem often affects marriages." At the ring of the phone, she jumped from her chair. "Be right back."

Her words lingered in his mind. How often had his mother tired of listening to his father's words, of his promises? Josh wondered.

"Hello? Hello?"

At Allie's insistent tone, he looked up.

She stood at the phone, frowning.

"Wrong number?" Josh asked, leaning against the terrace door.

"No answer. Some creep." Annoyance passed swiftly across her face. When she faced him, she wore her usual smile. "When I lived in Chicago and in Boston that happened often enough. But I didn't expect it in a town this size."

"Creeps live everywhere."

"More than likely it's one of the practical jokers at the station." Despite the calmness of her manner, when the phone rang again, she whirled around, snatched up the receiver, and offered a greeting that was filled with a demand. "Hello."

"Jeez! Hello," the voice grumbled back. "Don't yell."

"Neil?"

"Yeah. What's the matter with you?"

"You're lucky that you said hello this time."

"Huh?"

"Didn't you call a few minutes ago and do your famous Freddy of Elm Street deep-breathing bit?"

"No."

"Don't clown about this, Neil."

"I'm not. Did you get an obscene phone call?"

"A scuzzball."

Neil laughed. "You sound too sexy over the airwaves."

"Chauvinist. When was the last time you got an obscene phone call?"

"Don't I wish."

She rolled her eyes and leaned her hip against the kitchen counter. Then feeling Josh's stare, she turned her back to him. "So what did you want?"

"Junior told me to dig out the 'oldies but goodies' bunch."

"He'll bury this station yet."

"Could happen," he agreed. "But play them anyway."

"Right."

"That's the latest missive," he said on a snide laugh. "Bye."

"Bye," Allie responded quickly, aware he had only minutes between songs.

"Trouble?" Josh asked as she set down the receiver.

"We have a program manager who's out of touch. The radio station was almost ready for cremation when a new owner took over. However, he placed Junior, his son, in the program manager's job. Now, this is a college town. We have to appeal to a certain age group, and he wants us to play 'oldies but goodies.'"

"Some of the kids like the big band sound."

"Rock mostly. Junior doesn't know what to do to bring up our ratings, so he's scrambling around having us play everything. And why should he know? He's worked the past six years at one of the family-owned insurance agencies. KFKQ was a soft rock music station. During prime time, we're playing heavy metal. The afternoon deejay is playing whatever Junior decides would be good that day. Neil's playing the top forty."

"And you?"

"I'm the only one that Junior hasn't talked to." She laughed softly as she set dessert plates on the table. "There are advantages to being on the air when people are sleeping. But I play soft rock. I alternate between requests and 'music sets' so—" At the questioning tilt of his head, she explained, "Most of my air time is 'operator-assisted automation'. The music is on tape, and three to four songs are on the set. In between, I do promos or commercials. But during the day, anything goes at KFKQ. And now, he's just added the—"

"Oldies but goodies," he finished for her.

She smiled and gathered silverware from a drawer. "Yes. Disaster is about to hit."

"When did you start working there?"

"Only three months ago." She opened the bakery box and sniffed at the apple fritters. "I was underpaid or I'd have been axed, too."

"Layoffs?"

"Unbelievable ones." She set a fritter on his plate. "So many employees were let go with the change in owners."

"But not you. You must be good."

"Cheap." She licked sugar from the tip of a finger. "Having just started there, I wasn't getting an enormous paycheck so I could stay. I took over the nine-to-two shift after they let the previous deejay go."

"This fellow Neil—" Josh started to ask before cutting the fork into a fritter, "He's a deejay, too?"

She nodded, eyeing him. She would have preferred eating the fritter with her fingers. "He wasn't let go, either. Swinging Sam was."

His brows bunched.

She couldn't help but smile. "That was his moniker. With the changeover in management, he and several others were replaced.'' She made a face. ''Those are the breaks. But,'' she admitted, ''I never quite get past the feeling that I've nudged someone out of a job.''

''Did you?''

''Not really.'' She reached for a fork then dismissed the idea. ''Sam, specifically Sam's salary, proved dispensable.''

''And Neil?'' he asked again. ''Is he a friend?''

The fritter between her fingers, she took a bite and stretched forward to reach the kitchen counter and flick on the radio.

''This is Neil Compson at KFKQ.''

''He's on the air before me,'' Allie informed him, settling back on the chair.

Josh leaned forward to see what frequency she'd set the dial on so he'd know what station to tune in later. ''You never answered. Is he a friend?''

''Yes.'' She drew her legs up and propped her heels on the edge of the chair.

He'd noted that she rarely was still. As if pumped with high energy, even when she was sitting, she shifted often. ''That you date?''

''Occasionally. We're working friends.''

He wanted to kiss her. The thought sprang into his head without any warning. Mentally he swore at the sudden warming of his blood. She was interesting. Enticing. But not his type.

''If ratings don't go up, I suppose I'll be packing soon.''

''That doesn't bother you?''

She shook her head. "I love the traveling, the freedom."

"The grass isn't always greener over the hill." He personally knew that it could look just as dead and brown as the one behind him.

She ignored his comment. "So your first day of school wasn't a joyful experience?" she asked, watching him rub a hand across tired eyes.

"Should I admit to tension?"

"You'd sound normal. From some of the calls that come into the station from college students, Dean Forsythe sounds like a grouchy bulldog."

"He looks more disagreeable than he is." Josh grinned as he admitted, "He's the epitome of proper."

"You'll fit in."

Cocking his head, he frowned. "I'm not sure that's a compliment."

"I saw you leaving in your tweed sports jacket." She narrowed her eyes in a studying manner. "All you needed was the pipe."

"No pipe."

"In five years, you'll fit in perfectly."

The image she was conjuring wasn't pleasant to Josh. "Like an old shoe?"

"If that's what you want."

Annoyed, he bit into the fritter to rein his temper. "But not you?" he mumbled.

Her mouth full, she held up a finger while she quickly finished chewing. "I never want to feel tied down to anything or any place." Or anyone, she mused but kept the telling thought to herself.

"Why not?"

Allie stifled her usual candor. She had too many pride-stripping reasons to tell a perfect stranger about them. "I wouldn't have anything new to experience or learn," she answered instead. As if suddenly remembering an appointment, she gathered the napkins and the plates and stood. "Thank you for dinner."

Josh shoved back his shirt cuff and glanced at his watch. "Or breakfast."

On a laugh, she raked a hand through hair tousled from sleeping. "You're right. I haven't been up long."

He stared at eyes slightly hooded. "You still look good."

Wariness flashed into her eyes.

She whirled away and back into the apartment as if she were running from something—maybe him—he thought as he sat alone on the terrace. She didn't want to do this again, he realized. Though comfortable, an undercurrent of awareness had rippled through the air every time their eyes had met. He balled a napkin and shoved back his chair. He found her standing against the kitchen counter as if glued to it. "I'll leave now."

Her arms folded across her chest, she didn't move an inch. "Thanks again."

"Any time." Josh headed for the door. He wondered if she realized that merely thinking you want or don't want something didn't solve all of a person's problems. As a child, he'd wanted a home, a chance to make friends. And he'd learned that wanting something so badly that you ached inside for it didn't matter.

With a glance back, he noted that she hadn't moved. He didn't want to do this again anymore than she did, he realized. It wouldn't lead anywhere. But as he reached for the doorknob, he paused. From the kitchen, he heard her humming. She had a soft husky voice that beckoned, and he knew that he would be back.

Chapter Three

At six in the morning, Allie should have been home. Instead she crouched before the tape deck in the radio station and hunted through a storage bin for a Paula Abdul tape. A coward's streak urged her to stay at the radio station after her program. The less contact with her new neighbor the better. Something about the way he looked at her with those serious eyes made her uneasy. She'd ignored leers most of her life. Maybe, that was the problem. He hadn't leered. He'd just stared as if trying to see inside her. Definitely she didn't need to get involved with some intellectual who was hell-bent on analyzing her psyche.

As the phone rang on the counter above her, Allie nudged herself from her thoughts. With a roll of her shoulders against the tiredness grabbing hold, she offered a greeting. A hearty masculine snort answered her hello.

Neil sounded amazingly wide awake. "What are you doing? Why are you still there?"

Allie juggled the telephone receiver and then cradled it between her jaw and shoulder. "I decided to stay at the station and do my schedule here. What are you doing? Tracking me down?"

"Sort of."

"Next question." Incredulity slipped into her voice. "What are you doing up so early?"

"Something great happened yesterday."

"Did it?"

He responded with a laugh to her teasing tone. "And I have tomorrow evening off. So how would you like dinner before your airtime?"

Snatching the tape she'd been hunting for, she pushed herself to a stand. "A fancy dinner?"

"Not too fancy."

Picking up the cup she'd brought with her from the broadcasting booth, Allie stalled a second in answering while she took a sip of coffee. "I don't like Higley's Diner," she said, recalling the greasy spoon restaurant she'd tried on his recommendation.

He moaned. "Ah, Allie, give me a break. How was I to know that the health department was investigating them?" His voice brightened. "I can do better than that for you. But only prime-time deejays can afford fancy."

"You'll get a morning slot one day," she reassured him, knowing that's what he wanted most.

"Wouldn't you like to 'wing it' more?"

Cautiously she sipped the steaming coffee. "Morning shows are madness."

"And big bucks."

She settled her hips back against the counter. "I'm not goal-oriented."

"You should be, Allie. You have what it takes to make it big in this business."

"I'll leave 'making it big' to you," she answered distractedly, looking up in response to the sound of approaching footsteps. Standing in the doorway was KFKQ's newest employee. No more than twenty, Chad Senteno was tall and gawky-looking. Allie hadn't seen him smile once in the week and a half that he'd been working at the radio station. "Hold a second, Neil," Allie said, offering Chad a smile. As he returned an uncertain one, Allie guessed that shyness was his major problem. "Do you want something?"

"I'm—I'm— Do you want anything from the deli across the street?"

Allie shook her head. "No, but thanks, Chad."

"I could get you something to drink." Self-consciously he shifted his stance, but he never took his eyes off her. "More coffee or—"

At his insistence, Allie held onto her smile. "No, I really don't want anything."

On a frowning nod, he turned away and disappeared from the doorway as quietly as he'd appeared.

"I'm back," Allie said into the receiver.

"What was that all about?" Neil asked.

"Chad."

"I can't stand him. If he wasn't B.J.'s nephew, he wouldn't have gotten the messenger's job. Strange character."

"Shy," Allie suggested.

"Weird is a better word for him. And stuck on you, I'm afraid. He's probably going to make a real pest of himself, Allie."

"I'm not worried about him." She skimmed a new advertiser's hype about acne cream. "So what time for dinner?"

"About six-thirty. I'll tell you my good news then."

"No hints?"

A pleased laugh edged his voice. "Nope. I'll tell you everything tomorrow night."

Shaking her head, she muffled a yawn. "Can hardly wait."

"You'd better go home to bed."

"On my way."

At five that afternoon, the scent of bacon greeted Josh as he climbed the stairs toward his apartment. At the landing, he stared at Allie's door while he weighed his apartment key in his hand. He thought about the casserole dish of spaghetti in his refrigerator. While he was eating dinner, Allie was cooking breakfast. Even their lives were in opposition. He should go in and forget the woman at the end of the hall. His good intentions strayed as he stared at the package outside her door. Unable to decipher what it was, he strolled down the hall for a better look. Flowers, he realized from feet away. From someone special? Curiosity as much as neighborliness made him reach down for the long florist's box and then rap on the door.

He expected the door to swing open, instead, she called out, "Who is it?"

"Josh. Delivery."

"What?" The hint of puzzlement in her voice immediately slipped away. "Come in."

He pulled the door open. "I found—" Josh cut his words short and stopped dead in the doorway.

In a headstand against the wall, she smiled upside down at him. "I'll only be another minute."

She could take as long as she wanted. Leotards clung to her firm, long legs. Josh braced a palm against the doorjamb and enjoyed the view. "Do you do that every day?"

"Twice a day. Once at home and once at the radio station."

"While working?"

"No one can see me. I exercise to music, dance around," she said on a quick breath. "I'm alone there," she added while pushing her feet against the wall and then bounding to a stand. "Swinging Sam used to practice karate. But then he also rubbed the rotund belly of a Buddhist statue for good luck every morning."

Different people, Josh mused as his eyes roamed down her back. It was straight and slender, and her waist was small, her hips more angles than curves. As she faced him and stared expectantly at the florist's box in his hand, Josh snapped himself back with a quick shake of his head. "I don't know who they're from. I saw the box outside your door."

Her fair brows bunched. "I've been home a while."

"They were probably just delivered."

"Then why didn't the delivery boy knock on the door?"

Josh heard concern in her voice.

"Oh, well, who knows," she said with a shrug as she took the box from him.

He stood his ground, too curious about the flowers to move away. "Do you like flowers?"

"Every woman does." Tugging at the red ribbon wrapped around the box, she inwardly tensed with the shrill of the phone. Twice yesterday, the phone had rung and she'd been greeted with silence. With a quickness that prevented her imagination from grabbing hold and envisioning that some psychotic weirdo had memorized her number, she lunged for the receiver and offered a sharp, "Hello."

"Allison."

The stiff, crisp feminine tone stirred mixed feelings. Though grateful to hear a familiar voice, Allie rarely ended any conversation with her mother without gritting her teeth at least once.

"We're having a 'do.' I'm calling early because you told me last time that a week wasn't sufficient notice."

Instinctively Allie tightened her fingers on the telephone receiver. "What's it for?"

"I've been reelected for another term."

Tension eased from her and gave way to genuine relief. The phone call wouldn't focus on her. "How wonderful," she said honestly, aware of how hard her mother had worked during her campaign.

"Then we can expect you?"

"I'll try."

"You may bring a guest."

"I'm not—"

"Sarah is seeing a neurosurgeon now," she added before Allie could respond.

"Oh." Allie settled her hips back on the arm of the sofa and prepared herself for a lecture about marriage and settling down. "Sarah's not moving to North Carolina? To Spring Forkes?"

"Whatever for?"

Allie measured her words. "When I talked to her last month, Sarah said that she was considering leaving Boston and moving there."

"It would be foolish."

"She loves the country, Mother."

"Allison, be sensible. What kind of recognition, what kind of career would she have in some hick town? What possible reason would she have for leaving the medical center?"

Happiness, Allie thought, but doubted her mother would agree. "And this neurosurgeon? Does she care about him?"

"He might be ideal for her, and she certainly would be an asset to him."

She made it sound like a merger. But then her mother believed that if a marriage didn't provide benefits, why bother? Allie knew now her parents' marriage hadn't been based on love.

"And of course, Marilyn and Roger will be there. So we'll expect you," she said in a firmer voice.

Allie cringed. Even if she gathered courage and refused, her mother would remain calm and certain as always. And Allie would go anyway. "I'll try," Allie responded with good intentions even as she searched for an excuse not to be there. Her eyes shifted to the man standing in her living room. How much of the conversation had he listened to? How much had she revealed to a stranger in seconds that in her twenty-eight years no one in her family had seen?

By the time she set down the receiver minutes later, Josh had placed as much distance between them as possible to offer her privacy.

"My mother," she said, turning and facing him.

He ended his play with a picture frame filled with sand that shifted in liquid with the slightest movement. "Do you have a big family?"

"Two sisters. My father is a biochemist. My sister Sarah is a doctor. And my other sister Marilyn is a corporate lawyer at the same firm as her husband. And there are dozens of cousins. My family has roots as deep as sequoias. My grandfather had been a doctor at the same hospital that my sister practices at. My mother was born and raised in the house that she still lives in, and near the town where she presides as mayor now."

He deciphered no jealousy in her voice. She'd made the statements matter-of-factly, even proudly. She'd spoken about her childhood and her family with a casualness that puzzled him. He'd craved for the very background that she'd chosen to desert.

"My sisters have an abundance of admirable qualities. Good genes, my mother claims."

He heard it then. A faint edge of resentment? Or frustration?

"According to my family, I have redeeming qualities. I have great eyes." A laugh slipped into her voice. "But skinny hips."

He eyed them. They looked good to him.

"And—" She splayed her hands before him. "I have the shortest nails anyone has ever seen. I bite them, you know. That disturbs everyone. Everything I do does, so I rarely show up at family functions."

She stood before him in black leotards and an above-the-knee shirt with a yawning Garfield on the front of it. Without any makeup and her hair tousled, she looked far younger than a woman over twenty-five. At the college, he dodged female students, even some who looked older than she did at this moment. But then he'd never wondered about the perfume any of them were wearing. "What is it that you do that's so disturbing?"

"I didn't want to be a professional." She heard herself rambling but a nervousness consumed her. He had searching eyes. The kind that probed as if he were trying to see beyond her words. "I didn't want to marry one," she went on. "I didn't join the symphony. I balked and set my musical inclinations toward rock music and broadcasting. The day I announced my plans, my mother swooned, my father dropped his pipe and my sisters nearly fainted. I'm too far left to suit them," she added, lifting the white lid on the florist's box.

Josh moved closer. "Are you an accomplished musician?"

"I play at the piano." While she read the card, a puzzled look returned to her face.

He peered over her shoulder to read the signature on the card. "Secret admirer?"

Allie offered a careless wave. Since arriving in Barrington, she'd joined several of her co-workers at the radio station for dinner or bowling, but she'd dated no one. Puzzled, she frowned as she lifted the green tissue in the box. She thought few things could surprise her. She loved the unexpected, relished anything that was unusual. Usually. On a mirthless laugh, a nervous-sounding one even to her own ears, she pointed into the box. "Look."

He already was. "What do you make of that?"

She managed a small smile. "It might be someone's way of telling me that he thinks my program stinks?"

Josh stared at the brown, dried-out flowers. "Lousy sense of humor."

"An extravagant one. He paid a lot of money to let a dozen red roses die."

He caught the quick flash of distress in her face. "Must be a bad florist," Josh said, wishing for some way to ease her obvious worry.

"Must be."

She looked so confused. The wilted flowers had upset her and she kept forcing a weak smile as if it would bring life back into what now resembled weeds. Vulnerable, he thought. She looked so vulnerable that he wanted to draw her into his arms and assure her that the flowers were someone's crackpot idea of a joke. Instead, he jammed a hand into his pants pocket as he sensed that she wouldn't want such softness. She was battling it within herself. "Well—" he started but didn't move.

She looked at him with those large, blue eyes and he felt as if he were caught in some trance. He felt foolish. He wasn't some inept adolescent. He'd had his share of romantic encounters. For two years, he'd lived with a woman before they'd decided they wanted to live at opposite coastlines. The relationship had ended in a mature, amiable way, each wishing the other good luck. But he found himself standing with this woman and feeling as if he just realized how wonderful females were. "Are you working tonight?"

"Yes, I am."

To other women, he'd said goodbyes that had meant forever. Why couldn't he manage this one? He would see her the next day. And the next. But he couldn't get himself to walk out the door. Staring at the flowers again, he grinned wryly. "They look like something I'd grow."

"No green thumb?"

"No." His brows bunched with a feigned grimace. "And I became the adoptive parent of several drooping plants. But I haven't had the heart to toss them yet."

Grateful for something else to think about, she asked with genuine interest, "What kind of plants?"

"I don't know," he admitted.

"That's important."

"Is it?"

"Well, of course."

"Tomorrow—" He started to line up time with her even before he realized he was doing it.

She sighed heavily and breezed past him. "By tomorrow, they could be on their way to the great land beyond. I'd better look at them now."

"This is a Davallia griffithiana," she informed him minutes later as they stood in his living room. "A squirrel's foot, it's called. You can't stick this plant in the window. It needs filtered light." She turned her attention to another plant and fingered the brown tip of a leaf. "This one needs watering less often."

"How do you know so much?" he asked, more interested in watching the light dancing across her hair with her movement than learning about the plants.

Though he moved only a fraction of an inch closer, she could smell his woodsy aftershave. It was a reliably masculine scent. "I used to trail after the gardener. He told me all about plants."

Surprise crept into his voice. "A gardener?"

"We weren't all that rich. My mother was just too busy for domestic chores and needed a showplace for a home. So we had a gardener and a housekeeper twice a week."

"And where is 'home'?"

With her fingers, she clipped off a brown leaf from a philodendron. "Boston."

"Don't you want to work there?"

She faced him then. The eyes staring at her were too intense. With a look, the quiet and calm professor who lived his life in a world of books challenged every feminine instinct within her. Though she made her living at nonstop chatter, her voice locked. What was happening? she wondered as a sense of foolishness slipped over her. Forcing words forward, she spoke quickly, nervously even to her own ears. "I've worked in California, Texas, Montana, Idaho, Illinois. Lots of places."

Josh leaned back on the desk piled with teacher bulletins, his own personal homework from the college. He felt like sweeping it all in the wastebasket and spending the night with her. "Don't you get tired of drifting?"

"Moving around?" She shook her head. "I'd never want to be married to a job."

"So you're footloose and fancy free?"

Allie laughed while she pushed a finger into the moist soil of one plant. "I'm told that I have too much of my grandfather's blood in me. My mother's father. Much to my family's disapproval, he constantly told stories about his drifting days. He made his money in Alaska, drilling for oil," she added as an explanation. With the blink of an eye, her smile faded to a commiserating expression. "You nearly drowned this plant."

Humor flashed in his eyes. "How much water is too much?"

"This much is too much," she answered, but slanted a glance at him to see if he was laughing at her. When her family had finally acknowledged that she would never bend their way, they'd begun placating her and politely, smilingly tolerating her oddities. But the man beside her looked dead-serious now, his brows pinching with his frown. "It depends on how thirsty the plant is," she said more seriously, then clucked her tongue as her attention fell on the clay-like soil of another plant.

"For someone who enjoys plants, why do you have plastic begonias?"

A logical question from a logical mind, Allie thought. "Because I move too much," she said, sensing he would see the practicality in her answer.

"Why do you? To chase rainbows?"

His question seemed odd to her. "I never thought of it that way," she admitted. "Where are you from?"

"New Bedford originally. Then everywhere."

"Sounds exciting."

He responded to her smile. He couldn't ever remember smiling before when he recalled the never-ending moves during his childhood. Too many new schools. Too many new friends. And never the chance to feel comfortable with either. Yet, in hours, the woman standing near him had made him feel as though they were old friends. She made him feel a lot of things. If he wasn't careful, he would give in to an urge that had lingered within him ever since they'd met.

"Well, all your plants really need is TLC," she assured him.

"Just TLC? That's all?"

The sudden softness in his voice swiveled her face back to his. She could pretend that she imagined it. But one look in his eyes, and she would be forced to call herself a liar. Though she toyed with a familiar leaf, someone could have handed her a dandelion at that moment, and she would have called it a rose. "That's all," she answered.

With as much style as she could muster at the moment, she stepped away from him. When she reached the door, she made herself face him with a smile that veiled the turmoil inside her. She'd nurtured a similar smile through the years as protection to hide uncertainty, frustration and occasionally hurt whenever her lack of success became the number-one topic of conversation at family gatherings. "Take care of the plants," she said lightly.

"See you in the morning."

With a wave back at him, she rushed into the hallway. She would play smart from now on with Professor Joshua MacKenzie. She'd glue her feet to the floor of her apartment until after six, so she wouldn't see him in the morning. She had no answer for why she'd felt the quick warmth of desire flowing through her. She knew only that she wouldn't let that happen again.

Inside her living room, she bounded back into a headstand. He was likeable. He was also ambitious. People who worried about timetables usually were. She didn't need another high-achiever in her life, she told herself. He was too handsome to suit her. Too perfect. Too likely to remind her of everything she'd struggled for the past five years to forget.

Awakening to the sight of the black walls wasn't getting easier, Josh decided the next morning. Because of the nomad existence he'd known as a child, he'd learned to adapt to unfamiliar surroundings fairly quickly. So why was he feeling so restless this time? So damn unsettled? He swore softly at himself. An even bigger question was why couldn't he get the woman down the hall out of his mind? Was it possible that within a few days, one woman could inch her way beneath his skin? Crazy. He was thinking crazy.

Tucking his shirt into his pants, Josh waited for the final hiss of his coffee brewer. He poured himself a cup and eyed a cinnamon roll but strolled to the kitchen window instead. At nine-thirty in the morning, her car still wasn't parked at the curb in front of the house. Where was she? he wondered not for the first time since awakening.

The concern building within him for her worried him. It crossed the bridge of neighborly interest, of simple attraction. He never lied to himself. Honesty kept him on an even keel at all times. Flighty people made no sense to him. He'd yearned too long for predictability in his life to understand someone who liked their world topsy-turvy. But whenever he saw her, a tug existed, the simple man-woman response that nudged people closer. He wasn't adverse to commitment with a woman. After years of goals, he thought it was time that he found one—the right woman.

With only a half an hour to go before he left for work, he finished dressing. He didn't expect to see her, but as he knotted his tie, from the hallway, he heard laughter. It was airy and lighthearted, like her. It enticed him. He took a quick bite of the cinnamon roll then flung open the door.

Allie stood at the bottom of the steps, cradling a three-foot-high, stuffed giraffe by the neck. Juggling a stack of papers in her other arm, she dug into her purse for money. "I know there's money in here—somewhere. Thanks for delivering it so early." She smiled at the sleepy-looking adolescent before her.

He managed a nod. "We're an all-night pizza place." The carton tipped as he glanced at his wrist watch. "Are you eating this now?"

Nodding, she rummaged through her purse for several more seconds before she yanked out a bill. "Thanks again," she said, while making the exchange of money and pizza with him. Looking past the delivery boy, she saw Josh leaning against the banister. She felt too much, she thought. Too much excitement. Too much anticipation. Too much warmth. She veiled emotions quickly with an easy, "Hi, Professor. What are you doing? Playing hooky?"

Though she'd been up all night, she looked bright and wide awake. Her hair disheveled, her appearance was casual, just short of sloppy in snug jeans faded nearly white and a bright wine-colored sweatshirt suitable in size for a linebacker. "I have a late class." He gestured toward the panel of mailboxes. "I forgot to check the mailbox yesterday."

"It's being delivered already?"

"As soon as I was notified that the college had found an apartment for me, I got the address and notified the post office."

"Efficient."

He smiled wryly and wondered why he found her comment more insulting than complimentary.

Allie glanced at the one item sticking out of his mailbox. She hadn't seen a *Wall Street Journal* since she'd left home.

"Breakfast?" he asked, gesturing toward the carton when she joined him on a step.

Her eyes sparkled with amusement. "It's all in what you get used to. When I was little, I used to sneak into the kitchen before breakfast and get a can of tuna. It was for a stray cat that I had hidden in my bedroom."

The trace of a giggle in her voice gave her away. Climbing the steps with her, he squinted against a streak of sunlight spiking the hall and casting her face in shadows. Strands of her hair shone like sun-kissed silk. "But you let everyone believe it was for you, didn't you?" he asked.

"You're perceptive."

Her smile teetered between amusement and youthful whimsy. "My sister Marilyn was convinced that she was allergic to cats. If she saw one, she sneezed. I had that cat a whole month and not one sniffle." With a fingertip, she tapped the top of the carton. "Want some?"

He raised a hand as if warding off evil spirits.

"You should be more adventurous."

"Getting my stomach pumped isn't an experience I'm interested in."

"An exaggeration, Professor."

"Are there anchovies on it?"

"Yes."

He grimaced. "No exaggeration."

"Ah, you have a weak stomach."

"It likes to receive the right food at the proper time of the day."

Stuffy, she told herself. He was too stuffy for her, except when he laughed. He didn't do it often enough. Serious people rarely did. In a few years if he wasn't careful, he would be perfect as the rigid scowling professor dreaded by all. "I guess I'm more flexible. During my last job, I worked from four in the morning until nine. Before that it was seven at night to one in the morning. Maybe, my next job will be more normal." At the music floating out from his apartment, Allie tipped her head. "Mozart?"

Surprise flashed in his eyes. "Do you like Mozart?"

She giggled. "You expected me to be a musical retard, didn't you? You don't have to answer," she went on easily. "I won't put you on the 'hot seat.' I like Beethoven better. And Springstein," she added on a laugh.

As she tightened her grip on the giraffe's neck, he couldn't keep himself from asking. "What are you going to do with that?"

Because she heard a tinge of disapproval in his voice, she lied. "Oh, this is my new pet. I think that I'll call him George."

Josh narrowed his eyes at her. Was she really wacky enough to view a stuffed animal as a pet? Unsure what to say, he simply nodded his head.

Her eyes skimmed his starched, pin-striped shirt and perfectly knotted tie. "I'm keeping you. You'll be late," she said, taking the first move and whirling away from the eyes that had locked in a potent stare with hers.

The back of his neck prickled with tension. Waiting, he watched until her apartment door closed behind her. Then on a frown, he spun around and strolled back into his apartment. Slamming the cinnamon roll into the garbage can, he knew that he was angry for no reason in particular. If he had any good sense, he would back away from her. She was like a gypsy. She would flutter through his life and be gone. He preferred more lasting relationships. So why was she getting to him? He opened the closet door, wondering how the hell he would stay away from her.

With a glance at his watch, he strolled to the bathroom to retrieve his comb before he left for the college. Steps from the door, he heard the sound of rushing water and gritted his teeth. She had a lot of faults. A hell of a lot of faults. She hogged the bathroom. She was careless, not even locking her door. And messy, not knowing where in her purse to find her money. And what about that dumb giraffe? She was silly. Interesting. Fascinating. Fun.

Fun! When had fun mattered to him? He guided his actions in a serious manner. Though impatient by nature, he was also stubbornly tenacious. He'd learned to wait but he never gave up when he wanted something. He realized that to some people he'd listed what sounded more like faults than virtues.

Leaning a shoulder against the doorjamb, he listened to her singing at the top of her voice. What made her so interesting to him? Was it something so simple as pure physical attraction? Or was it the challenge she presented, the unpredictability she'd rush into his life? On a curse, he spun away and then strolled down the steps toward the door. Rational thinking was futile. With every step away, he felt a temptation to turn around, go back and spend more time with her.

For a man who prided himself on punctuality, he arrived at his medieval history class three minutes late. Though he wasn't prone to black moods, his edged toward a foul one when he entered the faculty lounge at eleven that morning. He'd had a stack of student papers to read last night, and he'd never taken them from his briefcase. He'd been daydreaming about her instead.

She'd been his last thought before going to sleep.

She'd been his first thought when he'd awakened.

She was constantly in his thoughts, intruding even during his lectures.

Because of her, he hadn't slept well, he hadn't finished that cinnamon roll and he'd been late for class. As he strolled toward the coffee urn at the back of the lounge, his stomach rumbled complainingly. Like the building's offices and hallways, the room echoed of old, established wealth with its oak-paneled walls, high-arched windows of beveled glass and gilt-framed oils.

Josh nodded to two professors from the English department. They acknowledged him, and then in hushed tones, they resumed their debate about defense spending. They represented the college: old, austere and dignified.

At the back of the room, news from the television set mingled in with conversations. Josh glanced at the fuzzy picture before eyeing the plate of powdered-sugar doughnuts nearby. In passing, he touched Nate's shoulder.

"I'd like you to meet someone," Nate said, stopping Josh in mid-stride.

Josh cast a longing look at the doughnuts but turned around.

"Noreen Dodd." Nate nodded toward an attractive woman. "Josh MacKenzie."

She was a pretty woman with a flawless complexion and brown hair. There was nothing wrong with her, except she wasn't the one he wanted to be with, Josh realized as he offered his hand.

"I've heard so much about you," she said.

His hand remained closed over her softer one, but he recalled Allie's firmer handshake. Her fragile hand had slipped in his but her grip had been decisive. When had a woman's handshake been something he considered for any length of time?

"I'm quite pleased to finally meet you."

Josh snapped himself back to the woman before him but knew he was staring dumbly at her.

"You'll be a welcome addition on the staff." Her smile warmed.

"Thank you," he managed.

"Noreen is head librarian," Nate informed him.

Why wasn't he pursuing a woman like this? Josh wondered. Why did his mind cling to the image of a certain slim blonde who denied wanting everything he needed in life? He couldn't rationalize any of his feelings for Allie but one—he wanted her.

"Noreen's father is Professor Dodd. Math department," Nate added.

"He teaches Analytic Equations. My mother also teaches here. Perhaps, you've met her. Professor Claydell. She teaches Business Statistics."

"I've met your father," Josh responded.

"Well—" She paused and smiled awkwardly. "It was nice meeting you."

"Yes, same here." As she strolled away, Josh whirled around to the plate of doughnuts.

Standing beside him, Nate handed him a cup of coffee. "I started to tell you that several of the faculty have decided on a new project. Like myself, they believe that you'd be great as the history chairman."

Josh sent him an indulgent grin before chomping on the doughnut. "Thank them for me." He slumped on a nearby brownish, tweed sofa and closed his eyes. A mistake, he realized as an image of Allie floated forward in his mind. He saw that million-dollar smile of hers. Her large, intelligent eyes. Her pert nose. He nearly smiled himself as he recalled that it wrinkled a second before her lips curved upward with an impish thought.

"Now, we aren't offering only our good wishes," Nate said, regrabbing Josh's attention. "We've decided to assist you in getting the appointment."

Josh opened one eye slowly. "Assist me?"

"Yes." Sitting on a heavily upholstered chair across from him, Nate hunched forward in a conspiratorial manner. "We've decided that your biggest hindrance is—"

"My age. Correction, my youth—which represents irresponsibility in the eyes of the mighty at Wainwright."

"Exactly. So we considered what to do about that problem. You need to get married, or at least, engaged. Everyone pigeonholes married men as more stable and responsible. Even car insurance rates drop for males when they get married."

Josh pushed up off his spine. Something warned him that he'd better pay attention.

"And if you were married, then you'd be viewed as the epitome of a typical Wainwright professor—settled, somber, and—"

Josh interrupted before he included stale in that description. "One problem, Nate. I'm not married. I'm not even engaged, and I haven't been here long enough to meet—"

"That's it," Nate cut in, jabbing a finger at the air as if pinpointing a spot. "You haven't been here very long. But we have. Decades," he added and frowned at his own comment. "And we know the young, available women in this and nearby towns. More importantly, we know which women are suitable to be a professor's wife. Women like Noreen have the right background."

Was there such a thing as the right and the wrong background? Josh wondered. If so, then for a professor, his was all wrong. Background meant nothing. He stifled amusement at how much importance everyone placed on it. His background included a father who'd dropped out of high school to play a saxophone in smoky bars. "Is there a list of qualifications?" Josh sent him a quick teasing grin.

"Don't make light of this, Josh. Some women fit in better than others," Nate answered seriously.

Fitting in had always been important to him. He'd spent most of his life measuring out time for studies, time for work, time for dates. All of that had been to reach one goal. The one he was reaching for now. But to choose a woman that way seemed too calculating. He'd never considered any qualifications for the woman he would marry except one—love.

"So we're going to help you. Now, if you don't care for Noreen, I have a cousin Irene, who has a daughter named Eunice."

"Hold it," Josh insisted.

"Josh, don't be resistant to this. The plan is a good one. It will help you. You want the chairman's position, don't you?"

Josh contemplated his question. At thirty-one, he would do almost anything to have such a position at a college as well-respected in the academic world as Wainwright. The prestige was secondary. For once in his life, he would have a sense of belonging. Slowly he nodded his head at Nate.

Nate's lips spread wide in a pleased grin. "You can see that I'm right. The right wife might cinch the position for you."

Josh laughed. "Nate, just because I want one doesn't mean that I'll find one."

"No, of course not. And you wouldn't marry some woman for this purpose, but you need to meet eligible women. And if destiny plays a hand in our lives, perhaps, you'll fall in love with one before the decision is finally made by Forsythe and the other not-so-wise-old-owls."

Josh considered the idea for a long moment. He couldn't take the idea too seriously, but he would appease his friend's well-meaning effort. What could he lose? he wondered. Nothing. "Eunice, huh?"

Nate nodded confirmingly. "Eunice. Now, I haven't seen her in some time, but she used to be a very pleasant woman. A tad serious, but pleasant and, as I said, she's extremely intelligent."

She sounded like the kind of woman Josh usually chose. Someone who knew more about Napoleon than his short stature and his propensity for sticking a hand in his jacket. "Why not?" Josh murmured, deciding that he needed some distraction from thoughts about the blond dynamite down the hall from him.

"The plan is sound, Josh. And—" His words trailed off, his attention shifting to the television screen. "Crazy," he said softly. "Crazy people."

Josh looked away from the deep lines crinkling from the corners of Nate's eyes and toward the television screen. Gathered before the camera with signs in their hands, children and adults waved and yelled out a barely decipherable chant.

His back to them, the news commentator went on, "A small group advocating the painting of garbage cans in the residential streets has gathered outside the mayor's office."

Nate chuckled low. "I love this kind of stuff." With his head, he gestured toward several of his colleagues. "They get beet red over any kind of demonstration."

"Paint them," a youngster on the screen chanted, raising his arm in the air. Next to him, a woman waved a bow.

Whirling away from the television, the head of the math department grumbled, "Bows on garbage cans. Fruitcakes. That's what they are."

Slowly a grin tugged at the corners of Josh's mouth as he spotted one woman in the crowd.

"What will someone think of next?" Nate said on a laugh.

"Rebel rousers," one of the English teachers murmured.

His companion nodded agreeably. "Who would campaign for such a thing?"

Allie, Josh thought, unable to stifle an amused smile.

Chapter Four

He was a fuddy-duddy. A pain-in-the-neck fuddy-duddy, Allie decided at five that evening as she entered the bathroom and saw that Josh had bought and hung a wicker shelf. All of her things—her brushes, sprays and cosmetics had been placed in a definite order by size on one shelf. With the same meticulous care all of his were on another shelf. She cursed the regimentation as she'd scrounged to find her makeup cleanser. Because the neatness annoyed her, she succumbed to an impish streak to get even. Before she left the bathroom, she deliberately set her hairbrush on his shelf.

If nothing else, she hoped her actions sparked the sense of humor she sensed was buried deep inside him. He was stingy with it and his smiles. A shame, she thought. He had a wonderful smile. Slow-forming, it curled the edges of his lips before it took shape and reached his eyes. She wondered why some people found smiling so difficult. It took less muscles than a frown. For that reason alone, she smiled often. Incurably lazy, she sought anything that was easier. And by nature, he would plunge toward anything waylaid with obstacles as if needing every step in his life to be challenging or stressful.

With more gusto than usual, she shoved the last load of clothes into the dryer. Slipping a blouse onto a hanger, she heard the sound of footsteps on the basement stairs. Mrs. Vanovitch often came down to chat about her grandchildren while Allie did her laundry. A greeting on her tongue, she looked over her shoulder.

With a laundry basket in his hands, Josh stopped at the bottom basement step. Allie swung her gaze back to the unfolded clothes piled in her basket. She would hang her cotton blouses to prevent more wrinkling then get the heck out of there.

As he moved closer, Josh noted that her back was straight, tense. For some reason, he received a tinge of pleasure in knowing that she wasn't as indifferent to him as she pretended.

"I'm almost done," she said with a glance at the dryer dial. It indicated her clothes were in the final spin cycle.

"Don't rush on my account." He leaned against the table and stared at her profile. She'd avoided his eyes ever since he'd descended the steps. Almost nervously she brushed a strand of hair away from her cheek with the back of her hand. Dressed in a beige-and-blue ski sweater and khaki-colored pants, she resembled one of the coeds on campus. Looking at her now, her expression pensive, her clothes less flamboyant, he had a difficult time visualizing her as the same woman involved in the screwy garbage can campaign.

Hurriedly and haphazardly she began squaring towels. "I noticed you bought something new for the bathroom."

Josh sent her an askance glance as he pushed aside her detergent bottle to set his basket on the table.

She stilled abruptly and turned a frown on him. "The wicker shelf."

"Oh. I thought it would be a good idea."

"For you. Not for me," she protested in a tone as noncombative as she could manage. "I don't want my things organized."

His brows bunched with a frown. "Why not?"

"I just don't."

"It'll save you time when you're getting ready for work."

Allie wagged her head slowly. "I don't want to save time."

Crazy. The woman was crazy, Josh told himself. "You do a lot of things just to make a statement, don't you?"

His perception tensed her.

"Such as eliminating ugly garbage cans."

"You heard?"

"I heard. It was on a midmorning newscast. And everyone has been talking about it ever since."

"Oh, good." As he arched a brow, she frowned. "Oh, you didn't mean that as encouragement, did you?"

"Why do you do things like that, Allie?"

"Like what?"

Her innocent act didn't faze him. "Bows on garbage cans," he said simply.

She ignored the deciphering quality in his voice. "Next week, we're painting them."

"You'll get arrested. Is that what you want?"

Her voice turned serious. "Why is it a crime to make things better."

"Because the town council doesn't want pink garbage cans."

"Red," she corrected.

"The color isn't the issue here. Why are you campaigning for such a—"

Her eyes dared him. "Such a what? Trivial issue? Frivolous cause?" She dumped a pile of unfolded clothes into her basket. "I don't have to worry about more important issues." Though her voice lowered, she mumbled loud enough for him to hear, "I know there are people like you who'll do that."

He wasn't sure if he should be amused or furious. He wasn't the oddball, the one out of sync with everyone else. He couldn't make sense out of his own attraction for her. He'd led a more serious life for a reason. He wanted a stability in his life as deeply rooted as the subject he'd studied and now taught. He could never live day in and day out with a woman who fluttered through life like a butterfly, uncaring about anything around her but the sweet smell of the next flower. But he hadn't passed an hour lately without thinking about her. She made him feel sixteen again. Sixteen, eager and aching.

Reluctantly Allie met his gaze. She hated outbursts, confrontations, arguments of any kind. "Why is everyone so rigid?" she asked softly.

He felt almost disappointed that the flare of annoyance no longer deepened the color of her eyes to a deep, dark blue. "There's something stable about rules and regulations. Anyway, rules are necessary."

With a shrug, she brushed aside his comment, deciding she wasn't fond of his unshakable professor tone. "If anything, painting those cans would remove an eyesore."

He smiled, able to comprehend her logic. That worried him. The woman acted outlandish and undisciplined. Was that the attraction? "What's next?" he asked, sensing she made a habit of silly causes.

"Save the axolotls," she answered without a trace of hesitation.

"The what?"

"Salamanders."

"I know what they are."

Of course, he would. Einstein junior, she mused.

"I wasn't even aware that there were any here. Habitat is Mexico and the western United States," he said as if pulling the information from some computer source. Frowning, he added, "But I've never read of any being in Vermont."

Allie mentally groaned at the serious direction the conversation was taking. "No, there aren't any in Vermont," she assured him.

"I didn't think so."

"But when I was at the grocery store several weeks ago, a woman told me that they're becoming extinct."

"Therefore, save them?"

"Therefore, yes." Anything else she might have said was forgotten as he began refolding one of her towels into threes. "What are you doing?"

"I'm being helpful."

"No, you're refolding my laundry," she corrected.

"Well, they're folded—"

"Wrong?" she finished for him.

He raised his eyes. "If you fold the towels this way, they'll fit in that mouse-size linen closet we have. I checked."

"Checked?"

"I measured the shelf, then measured the largest towel I had and this is the most economically space-saving way to fold a towel."

She laughed because he looked so serious.

"What's so funny?"

"You sound so much like my family. They all believe everything has a proper place."

He arched a brow, not finding anything she was saying about them as peculiar.

"You, too?"

His frown deepened. "What's wrong with that?"

"You waste more energy doing all your calculations."

"Not really," he cut in. "Over a period of time, you'll save time and energy."

Amusement slipped into her voice. "How did you come to that conclusion?"

"You can grab a towel quickly this way."

She gave her head a slow shake. "I do anyway," she answered. She preferred men who took life less seriously. Men who acted spontaneously. Men who knew how to enjoy life.

"But you must pull other towels out so they—"

"So, it's a little messy?" She shrugged. "So what?"

He seemed to wince.

"Never mind," she said on a laugh. "I believe you. I lived my whole life with these kinds of discussions."

"What are they like?" he asked.

"Who?"

As she bent forward, strands of her hair fell across her cheek. He sidestepped an urge to bury his hand in the tousled softness of her hair. "Your family."

That look was in his eyes again. A questioning look as if he were determined to understand her. No one else ever had. Why did he want to? "I come from a family of overwhelming people," she said on a sigh, deciding a good honest talk would be best for both of them. "Intelligent, ambitious and disturbingly nice people. If I disliked them, life would be easier. But I care about all of them. I just can't be like them. They're high achievers. They demand a lot from themselves and anyone they come in contact with. In comparison to my sisters, the whiz twins," she said with an affectionate tease, "I was fluff. I was a cheerleader, not a member of the science club or a student body president." He kept staring at her as if trying to see beneath her words. Allie thought that they were revealing enough. "I did it all. All that was expected of me. I took ballet lessons and preferred tumbling. I hammered at the piano and attempted to learn the violin. I attended a private girl's school," she said while removing her clothes from the dryer. "But when they mentioned Julliard—"

"Julliard?" he cut in.

She wiggled her fingers in the air. "I play a mean piano. But when they wanted me to go to Julliard, I went to the state university instead. I even had a brief engagement to a man they approved of. Fortunately the fiancé went one way and I went another."

She was a restless spirit, someone who'd had no more of a sense of belonging than he'd ever had, Josh realized. So why did she thumb her nose at everything he'd yearned to have most of his life? "Rebelled every step of the way, didn't you?" he asked, remembering how hard he'd tried to adapt after every move.

"I never thought of it as rebelling," she answered as she placed her detergent bottle on top of the clothes.

With a glance at it, he noted that she hadn't folded half the clothes. They were stuffed in the basket. From what she'd said, he would find more common ground with her family than her. To some extent, she'd pigeonholed him accurately. He needed orderliness and certainties in his life. He sought continuity. She generated change. She rushed everywhere as if afraid she'd missed something. He strolled, wanting to absorb everything. He didn't need to get involved with a woman who was so opposite him, a woman who was determined to live a butterfly's life.

As she turned her head to step away, he swore at himself. No matter what his head told him, she was the one he wanted. It was his last conscious thought before his hand curled over her arm to stop her. Analyzing why he craved her taste was impossible. He knew only that a warmth was spreading through him.

When his eyes flicked to her mouth, all the warnings she might give herself later wouldn't come forward. She'd been wondering about his kiss. The professors she'd known had never emanated 'sexy.'

With one gentle hand at the back of her neck, he held her still. She didn't think to turn her face from his. As she drew a quick breath, his mouth grazed then pressed against hers. His kiss wasn't what she'd expected. His mouth moved over hers slowly, savoringly. A warm, sweet lethargy seeped into her. In seconds, her pulse pounded harder, and her body hummed. She thought the kiss would be quick, but the firm, hard lips pressing against hers captured her mouth in a long, lingering kiss that insisted she part her lips and not only respond but invite. She tasted too much experience, too much passion. In a seduction that kindled a warm pleasure through her whole body, his tongue caught and challenged hers.

Had she really believed that he lacked spontaneity? That he couldn't surprise her? Stun her? she wondered. Persuade her? Relentlessly his mouth moved over hers, insisting and demanding response. She gripped his shoulders, urging him, while her heart thudded beneath the gentle hand barely touching her. Why couldn't he have kissed her with the same stiffness that he led his life?

She tried to think clearly. But when had a man's kiss invaded the sheltered part of her heart? Why did he make the promise of passion seem so urgent? So exciting? And so dangerous to everything she believed in?

Though she recognized that danger building, she didn't pull away. Her body rested against his, her rounder softness cushioned by his angles. She trembled that with a gentle demand, his mouth made her yearn for more. She felt desperate to absorb every sensation as a need whipped through her. Sharp and swift and demanding. Even while she relished his taste with her lips, a greediness hastened her. She'd always thought that she hungered for nothing, yet she wanted more of the firm mouth seducing hers. With nothing more than a touch and a kiss, he rooted her to the ground. Impossible, she thought. She'd never wanted to be rooted anywhere, ever.

She murmured a protest against his lips. It was a protest, wasn't it? she wondered, yet seconds passed before she broke free, before the quickened beat of her heart slowed down, before a tenuous control returned. "You're full of surprises, Professor," she managed unevenly. With a breezy movement, she grabbed her basket and whirled away, determined that he wouldn't see how much he'd affected her. "Ciao," she called back. She hadn't wanted his kiss, she told herself. He'd had no effect on her. Her legs weren't heavy. A weakness wasn't flooding her body.

Halfway up the stairs, honesty slammed at her. Who was she kidding? She'd wanted him to kiss her, and the professor had proved that he was no slouch as a kisser. What a mess, she thought as she closed the basement door behind her.

He treasured everything that she'd strived to get away from. He needed organization. He demanded excellence of himself. He welcomed rules and regulations. He willingly led a life so predictable that it had to border boring. He was striving, aiming for success as if no other path existed. He was all wrong for her.

Hadn't he carefully and neatly stacked towels in her laundry basket? And what about the wicker shelves in the bathroom? He was a fussbudget. A handsome, ambitious, incredibly sexy-looking, fussbudget who she was having enormous difficulty resisting. That was all she felt. He liked things in their proper slots. He would want a woman who would fit in one, too. She never had. She never would.

He had to grin. If his breathing wasn't steady, neither was hers, despite her casual act. She was a woman with her own mind. He'd seen that instantly. She'd taken charge of a touchy moment when she'd opened the bathroom door on him. She wouldn't allow any macho muscle tactics, and he wasn't prone to demonstrate them. But how could he not have wondered if a woman so sunny, would also be warm? When he'd pushed his tongue past her teeth and into the heat of her mouth, he'd heard her soft moan and had wondered about stirring a deeper sounding one from her. At the moment, he could barely remember anything but the taste of her. Promising. Intoxicating. Sweet. He hadn't expected it to be so sweet.

When she'd turned away as if the kiss hadn't stirred her, he'd wanted to grab her, kiss her again and make her admit that nothing was casual about their kiss. He groaned softly, not believing how foolish he seemed even to himself. He'd known other women who were more beautiful, more intelligent, easier to talk to. They'd all made more sense to him than she did. Perhaps part of his interest in her evolved from wanting to learn what made her tick, uncovering the eccentricities, seeing her smile, hearing her laugh.

By the time he strolled toward his apartment, he'd given up analyzing. They had nothing in common, he told himself firmly. But one day he would kiss her, and she wouldn't walk away so easily. He promised himself that.

He reached the landing to the sound of his phone ringing, and on an oath, he raced to answer it. Slightly winded, he dropped the basket just inside his apartment and managed a breathless hello into the telephone receiver.

"Out of condition?"

Josh sank onto the sofa. The feminine voice was one he'd needed to hear at that moment, a reminder of why he'd vowed to make a permanent place for himself somewhere. "Mom, hi."

"Don't tell me you're exercising?"

"Forced exercise," he quipped. "I'm living in a second-floor apartment."

"Lots of stairs are good for you."

"Thank you." He scowled, eyeing the clothes that in his haste he'd toppled from his laundry basket and now were strewn across the floor.

"So, tell me," she said in a less maternal tone, obviously satisfied that she'd fulfilled the necessary motherly concern she started every phone call with. "Are you happy there?"

"I'm not settled in yet."

"Well, you know whether you're happy or not, don't you?"

Her question seemed ironic. If happiness was so important, why hadn't she worried more about her own for years? "I'm glad I decided to accept the position."

"So it's all that you'd hoped it would be?"

"It's nice to be back. And I have a good chance at the department chair position."

"I know how much you want the chairmanship. You do, don't you?"

"It would mean a lot to me."

"It isn't too—well—too quiet for you? You're used to more change in your life."

For too long, he'd waited for an opportunity like this one. For a place like Barrington. "It's what I want," he said firmly.

"You sound happy. And that's what I've always wanted for you."

"I know that. Enough about me. How are you?"

A laugh slipped in to her voice. "Oh, I have a new student. A gentleman."

Josh heard more than humor in her voice. "How old?"

"Oh, Josh."

He laughed. "Mom, how old is he?"

"Around my age."

"And he's taking piano lessons?"

"Cello." A girlish giggle slipped into her voice. "He was a pilot. He's retired. And he said that he's always wanted to play the cello, but until now, he's never really had the time."

"And what else?"

"What makes you believe there's anything else to say?"

Without seeing her face, he knew a soft pink hue had brightened her cheeks. She was a tall, slim, youthful looking woman with a hint of gray in her dark hair. For years, her eyes had been clouded with worry and tiredness, but with a whispered word or two, his father had always been able to stir a brightness to her eyes and a youthful blush to her face. She was a soft woman with a gentle heart who willingly gave whatever she could to others. Often, Josh had thought that she'd given up too many of her dreams.

"His name is Frank," she admitted reluctantly. "Frank Searson. That's all I'm telling you since I'm not allowed to ask you certain questions."

"Okay, I won't ask more for now."

"I'm so glad to hear that since I show you a similar courtesy. If you want to share stories about the latest love in your life, I might talk."

"Forget it."

"No lovely woman there who sets your heart pounding and will make me a grandmother soon?"

"You sound like everyone else here." Josh stretched out his legs and plopped his feet on the coffee table. "Nate—you remember him, don't you?"

"Oh, yes."

"He's trying to help me find a wife. He insists it's a nudge in the right direction."

"And you're going along with that? I'm amazed. You rarely want anything that comes easy to you."

"I'm not taking it seriously."

"Ah, I was right then," she said, sounding pleased. "No doubt, you have your eye on a more reluctant lady. No, don't bother answering," she said all in one breath. "Time will tell."

He chuckled.

"You said that you have a second-floor apartment. Is it nicer than that one you had in New York?"

"More than one room."

"Then it's nice," she said in an assuming voice.

His eyes swept around the apartment. "It's different."

"But nice and homey?"

He focused on a cushion of the shoddy green sofa. For days, he'd planned on shopping for new furniture. "Yes, it is," he answered. As she went on about her latest students, Josh noted that she carefully avoided mentioning Frank again. He settled back and laughed at her anecdotes. She sounded happy. He was glad. She deserved happiness. Both of them had endured more than they should have. Slowly he scanned the room and smiled. He felt happier, too. Oddly he hadn't thought about his discontent with the apartment in days, about much of anything—except Allie.

An hour later, while he was dressing for dinner at the Henderson's, his thoughts swung back to her again as he heard her voice in the hallway. Determinedly, he planted his feet before the dresser mirror while he knotted his tie. But when she laughingly said the name Neil, Josh couldn't keep himself from wandering to the window to see the man who'd stirred such warmth into her voice.

He watched her stroll toward a red Camaro with a blond man. After dinner the night before, Josh had tuned in the radio station and caught Neil Compson's broadcast. The guy sounded as if he had an overblown ego. Watching him now, walking too close to Allie, his hand proprietarily gripping Allie's arm, Josh had another impression of him. The guy was a jerk.

Possibly, he was, too, he decided later that evening as he sat beside Eunice on the sofa in Nate's home. Though he made every effort to enjoy the prearranged date with her, he struggled for smiles. She was a thin woman with glossy, dark hair that hung like a shiny mop. She was intelligent—but boring. For the past ten minutes, she'd droned on about the research she was doing in circadian rhythm and discussed the patterns of leaf movement. "Plant life is interesting, don't you agree?" she asked encouragingly to stir conversation from him.

He made a polite attempt. "Mine are half dead."

Nate snorted a laugh. "I never had much luck with plants, either."

Picking up his beer glass, Josh met Nate's eyes while Eunice informed them, "Plants thrive with a ten to fifteen degree difference in temperature, but a rapid change such as thirty to forty degrees will prove extremely traumatic."

"But with a little TLC," Josh teased, "they'll—"

Her lips pursed slightly and she shook her head. "Joshua, you surprise me."

Josh sent a puzzled look at Nate.

"TLC?" Eunice tittered. "Such a strange solution for such an intelligent man."

He vowed not to yawn before he left Eunice at her door. But when he got home, he would give those plants TLC. That's what they needed. Him, too.

"Try your hand at *Asteroids*," Neil suggested.

Allie set a hip against the pinball machine. "I thought we were going to a movie."

"Ah, Allie, what fun is there in sitting at a movie theater. I'm a doer, not a watcher. You, too, right?"

She nodded but then wondered why she was standing and watching a screen with its simulation of multicolored rocks bombarding a spaceship.

"Good," he said, his eyes tranced to the screen. "Because something happened the day before yesterday that I really wanted to talk to you about."

To her amazement, he let a giant boulder smash into the ship. *Game over* flashed across the screen. "Finally I'm going to hear your announcement."

"And it's great," he said, facing her. "A new radio station in Los Angeles is looking for deejays."

Walking with him toward the exit of the dark, noisy world of the pinball freak, Allie guessed where the conversation was headed. "You're going to leave KFKQ then?"

"I can't leave without a job secured somewhere else. But I'd sure love to get that Los Angeles job and get out of this hick town. I want to be noticed. Rich and famous," he said, flashing his pearly whites at her.

"What are your chances?"

"Better than average. Although it might not be permanent," he added.

"Our job rarely is."

He nodded agreeably. "But it could lead to another job in Los Angeles. And that's where I want to be."

"Sounds great," she said because she knew that's what he wanted to hear.

"Yeah, and they seem to want me," he said without a trace of modesty. "But I can make even bigger bucks with a partner."

Allie squinted against the bright lights of the shopping mall.

"They have a single late-afternoon slot open. And they have a morning slot—prime time, Allie. But the station wants a team, male and female, for the morning program." He paused suddenly and touched her shoulder. "Us."

Allie halted in mid-stride. "Us?"

"We'd be great together."

"They want names for their morning lineup, Neil."

"They've heard of you, Allie. They remembered when you used to work in California. They heard you when you filled in on a Los Angeles morning slot for the deejay who got stuck in that rainstorm. They liked your sound. And they like mine," he added with a wink. "We'd be perfect together."

Allie drew a long breath. Some people had phobias about high places or airplanes or dogs. She felt ready for an anxiety attack whenever she heard the word perfect. Panic slithered through her. If she didn't calm down, she would end up standing in the middle of Barrington's main street with her head between her legs to prevent herself from fainting.

"It's something to think about Allie."

She did through the rest of the evening. She liked her job, she reflected as she sat in front of the radio station console and announced the next song over the microphone. "This is KFKQ with more of your favorites, new and old. Now, something for that special someone in your life." As Barbra Streisand's voice rang out words about "people needing people," Allie sat back with a cup of coffee.

Neil was offering her a chance to make it big in the business. Why did the idea scare the daylights out of her? she wondered.

Why did the idea of packing up and moving on seem less enticing this time?

Why couldn't she stop thinking about a good-looking history professor?

The clock showed ten thirty-five when Josh opened his apartment door. Nate had sent him an apologetic look before they'd parted.

"Sorry about the disastrous evening, Josh," he'd whispered with a hand on Josh's shoulder. He'd glanced back at the loquacious Eunice bending Nate's wife's ear. Edith continued to smile and nod, but both men had noted that she was at a grin-and-bear-it stage.

"I enjoy being with you and Edith," Josh had said honestly.

Nate's grip had tightened on his shoulder. "I haven't seen Eunice since she got her doctorate. You never know if the degree will turn them into boring pinheads who've forgotten how to laugh. Don't despair. We'll find you another."

"Nate, maybe, we should forget this project that you've thought up."

"Now, son, just give it another try. You can't let one bad evening reflect on the success of my idea. That's not fair."

Josh had nodded agreeably for his friend's sake. Nate would introduce him to a well-groomed, intellectually stimulating, proper woman. A woman who was perfect for a professor's wife. A woman who might help him get Allison Gentry out of his mind.

He'd managed a fast goodnight to Eunice and then had driven back to his apartment. He could recall worse evenings. He'd also had better ones.

He strolled into the bathroom. A tornado had hit. Uncapped cosmetics lined the left side of the sink. His half, the right side, had shrunk noticeably, moving his jar of baking soda, his glass, and his toothbrush to the edge of the sink. Her hairbrush was back on his shelf. Thrown over the shower rod were pale blue lacy nothings that sent his mind racing and his libido into full drive.

Chaos had entered his life.

He brushed his fingers across the lacy trim of a bra then whipped around and out of the bathroom. On a curse, he slammed the apartment door and wondered if he was going crazy. She would drive him crazy. What was worse? A dull, boring evening with the brainy, compatible Eunice? Or the excitement of his blond neighbor who lived her life without a care in the world about any moment but the present one?

Josh flicked on the radio and heard her sultry voice.

Low, huskily, Allie announced the next song. A request. "This is a favorite one of Mr. and Mrs. Peter Vanovitch. Lionel Ritchie's 'Endless Love.' Happy anniversary Mr. and Mrs. V."

Josh settled back on the chair and smiled. Desire, quick and sharp, shot through him whenever he was near her. Even the sound of her voice had a startling warm effect on him. He wanted to make love with her, but the nudge of passion could be ignored. What he was having a hard time resisting was this need that was almost as intense to learn more about her. A yearning filled him to hear her voice, to see her smile.

He reached for the telephone and dialed the phone number that he'd looked up hours ago.

"KFKQ. What song would you like to request?"

"Do you take requests from neighbors?"

She was quiet for a long moment. "Josh?"

"Hi."

"Hi, yourself."

He heard her smile and settled back. This was what he'd been wanting to do all night. Hear her voice.

"What song?"

"Something suitable."

"For a professor?"

"For a man alone, listening to a beautiful woman's voice over the radio."

"Professor—" Pleasure, surprise, a tease mingled into her voice. "The song's almost over. What would you like to hear?"

"'Can't Get You Out of My Mind.'"

She was quiet again.

"Did you hear me?"

"Yes. It's an old song. I'll have to hunt for it."

"Try to find it," he requested softly.

She was silent.

"That's fair," he told her in a light, amused tone that clearly indicated laughter at himself.

A reluctant smile warmed her voice. "Is it?"

"Yes."

"Why is it?" she asked almost warily.

To hell with logic, Josh decided. All the sound reasons why he shouldn't get involved with her failed to make sense. Honesty forced an admittance from him. "Because I've been thinking all night about you," he said softly.

Chapter Five

Her heart hammered while she listened to the song's final notes. Who'd have expected the professor to be a romantic? Likeable. Handsome. Intelligent. All of that and more. But romantic? Never.

Professors weren't romantic or adventurous. They didn't make a woman's heart pound except in the movies. Or did they? Had Indiana Jones rummaging around in archaeological digs and thwarting off evil mongers killed that notion? Or was the staid, boring man with glasses and his nose buried in a book a stereotypical image that had never existed?

She'd assumed Professor Josh MacKenzie was from the same mold as her ex-fiancé Kyle Tollister and the members of her family. Life was serious. Reasons were practical. Decisions were made. Commitments were necessary.

She'd been the wrong kind of woman for Kyle. He refolded instead of balled his napkin. He lined up his shirts by color in his closet. He wouldn't think of doing something so trivial as rolling around in autumn leaves or building a snowman. Like her family, he'd admitted that he didn't believe in something as whimsical as romance. He'd had his life mapped out. He'd calculated that in so many years and months, they would marry. He'd had aspirations of a private practice in medicine. Who better to marry than the daughter of the biochemist who'd had a wing of a hospital named after him? He could have been cloned from her family. Josh, too, she'd thought—until he'd requested that song.

Why wasn't he fitting into the proper slot? she wondered. He was intense about everything, even bathroom schedules. He was bound by rules and sought commitments, but he wasn't predictable. On a sigh, she slid in a cassette for the next commercial. She had a long night ahead. Hours. Hours to think about him.

By midmorning of the next day, she still hadn't gotten him out of her mind. Like some adolescent, she caught herself daydreaming about him.

Annoyed and confused, she even resorted to making a checklist of things to do. The last time she'd written such a list was when she'd been twelve years old. She'd accomplished nothing on the list and had decided then that she wasn't a planner. Spontaneity suited her best, so she went with spur of the moment plans. If he had her doing something so uncharacteristic, then she definitely was in trouble. And if he kept popping into her life unexpectedly, she would sink deeper.

No, she wouldn't.

She would remember that his disciplined, controlled side could inch its way forward at any time. She would remember that he thrived on the predictable and sensible. Hadn't her hairbrush been placed back on her shelf in the bathroom? He felt compelled to keep things neat. Not that she had anything against neat. Neat was okay, but regimentation would drive her crazy.

She preferred a sense of the ridiculous in her life. And while he would impose some order on her life, she'd feel just as driven to loosen up his with trivial nonsense that would either infuriate him or arouse his exasperation. She was prone to do that to her family.

With the grocery store in mind, she slid on a heavy tweed jacket and plopped a hat on her head. She couldn't help wondering what his reaction would be when he found her hairbrush and her toothpaste pump on his shelf again. He would scowl, she decided. Maybe, grit his teeth. Or curse. Whatever he did, he'd have to realize what she already knew. They would never blend. But what if he didn't? On second thought, maybe, she did need some kind of plan.

By the time she finished carefully choosing fruits and vegetables and loading her grocery cart with twelve pumpkins, she hadn't thought of one shocking idea, of anything really weird, or of anything that would rattle his sense of propriety and make him back up a step or two.

Yawning, she pushed her cart past the meat counter. Instead of worrying about how to outfox Josh, she should have gone to the BBG, the newly formed Barrington Beautification Group, but she'd forgotten about the meeting.

At the radio station, everyone was on edge, unsure if they would have a job in a month. They'd gathered over coffee and discussed possibilities, all of which were assumptions ranging from everyone losing their jobs to KFKQ being promoted grandly and becoming number one in Barrington.

Allie accepted the uncertainty. She'd taken the job in Barrington because she'd remembered the beauty of autumn in the East. That seemed as good a reason as any for being in Vermont. She never doubted that she might be staring at palm trees or some antebellum plantation next fall. She liked the loose life-style, the freedom to go whenever she wanted or wherever she wanted. Life was an adventure of new places and new faces. But during an honest, quiet moment, she admitted to herself that she would like to spend Christmas, too, in Vermont. The peacefulness of the countryside, the quaint old inns, the unhurried pace appealed to her. Even grocery shopping in Barrington was an experience.

Where else but a small town could a person still find a Ma and Pa store? Established nearly a century ago, Bowman's Market had remodeled but strived to hold on to its original concept of selling homemade jams, bakery goods and sausage. It was a family-owned operation. Success had taken a second place behind quality. The people were friendly, and the owner, the grandson of Henry Bowman, though young, maintained the same ideals. Adam knew everyone by first name who entered his store.

A stroll down the aisle of stacked canned goods often provided a lengthy social visit with a neighbor. Everyone knew everyone in Barrington. Everyone was a neighbor.

Everyone, she reflected as she turned down the next aisle with its shelves of condiments and stood face-to-face with Josh.

She allowed herself only a fraction of a second of pleasure at seeing him again, intending to nod hello and push past him. Even that simple plan failed. With a glance downward, she caught herself smiling. While she'd filled the upper portion of her cart with plastic bags of fruits and vegetables, Josh's contained the gourmet delights of a ten-year-old. "You believe in mistreating your body, don't you?"

His gaze followed hers to the Twinkies. "I believe in self-indulgence." After the kiss they'd shared, her casualness annoyed him.

Allie deliberately chose her next words. "For someone who's so persnickety about time schedules—"

He curled his fingers over the front of her cart, preventing her from pushing it forward. "Persnickety?"

Though her intent was to send him off irritated at her, at his affronted look, laughter edged her voice. "I meant—"

He raised a halting hand. "Don't bother. I know exactly what you meant."

"I'm really sorry," she said, feeling the inevitable softness surfacing. "I didn't mean to insult you, but—" As his frown deepened, she couldn't hold back a laugh. "I'm sorry. I'm really sorry. But you're scowling."

"And that's funny?"

"Well, yes."

"First, I'm persnickety. Then a scowl that I have, may I add, worked hard to perfect to scare the daylights out of my students is funny."

Despite his serious tone, his eyes sparkled with humor. She'd always liked people who could laugh at themselves. She hadn't expected him to be one of them. "I never would have taken you to be a junk food addict. How can you do something so criminal to your body?" She bent over his grocery cart. "Cookies. Chips. Spice drops. Ooh." She grimaced. "Gooey caramels. Do you know what they do to your teeth?"

"It's better than what you do to your stomach by eating seaweed," he countered with a nod of his head toward her cart.

"That's kelp."

"It's seaweed."

"But healthy."

"How boring," he quipped on a grin. "Anyway," he said, frowning at her cart full of pumpkins, "what are you on? A pumpkin diet? What are you going to do with those?"

"Carve them."

"They'll fall apart within the week. Why get so many?"

She was tempted to bait him, but she decided it might lead to more time together. She couldn't afford more than a quick encounter. "They're not for me."

She scooted around the corner as if they were giving the food away in the next aisle. Josh wasn't easily dissuaded. Following her, he found her engrossed in reading the ingredients on a cereal box. "For whom, then?" he asked.

"They're having a Halloween magic show at the children's hospital. I volunteered to carve some pumpkins for it."

Her answer unsteadied him. He expected a nonsensical one. His mother often had done something similar. No matter where they'd lived, she'd involved herself in the community. He inclined his head and studied the impish face of the woman before him, certain not for the first time that she wasn't what she seemed to be. His gaze flicked up her baggy beige pants, the pink and green scarf draped over a shiny fuchsia blouse visible through her open jacket, and the fedora-styled hat. She dressed weirdly, yet she always looked attractive. She countered everything he believed in and fascinated him like no other woman ever had. "How do you plan to get all of those home?"

"I'll manage."

"I could help."

Allie felt her pulse jump like a warning. For once in her life, she refused to be a soft touch. She considered that trait her biggest fault.

"Repayment," he added. "I never thanked you for playing my song." As she frowned slightly, he tapped a finger at the box she was holding. "What's the matter? Too much sugar?"

"No, I was thinking about your request. I'm not supposed to be taking any," she admitted.

"Then why are you?"

"People like to make them. Fortunately no one in management has told me to stop yet, so I keep doing it."

"Conforming isn't considered a sin," he teased.

She slanted a wary look at him, sensing he was leading her into a verbal trap. "No, but if it exists all the time, it can be dull. Excitement keeps the mind alert," she said, bending forward for a different box of cereal. As she straightened, she found herself too close to him.

"Excitement can be found in a lot of ways," he said softly.

His breath fluttered across her face like a reminder. As a quiet challenge stretched between them, she admitted the desire that he aroused but assured herself it could be ignored. Foolish thinking, she decided, as for one long moment, he riveted her to the spot with a look. On an unsteady breath, she nudged herself to move away. The quiet, unassuming professor with his conventional attitudes was dangerous. Quickly she stepped around him to reach the bakery display counter. "I love this store," she went on, determined to share nothing more than inconsequential conversation. "Where else can you get homemade streusel coffeecake."

He'd seen vulnerability. Though he'd always considered himself a man in control, he'd felt weak for those few startling seconds, weak to hold her, assure her that he wouldn't hurt her, and he didn't know why. While she drew a deep breath to absorb the sweet scent of the cakes, he inhaled the sultry fragrance she wore. "So you have a sweet tooth?"

"A little one," she said, eyeing the fudge brownies.

"Hey, Josh." Adam Bowman, a tall and lean man with a trim dark mustache was known to have three loves: his family, his store and skiing. "You'll think about what we discussed, won't you?" Adam asked in passing.

"I'll see how my schedule goes."

"We need a hotdogger," he returned on a laugh.

"I'm getting older."

"Ah, the downfall of recklessness," he quipped before turning away to stock a coffee display.

Perplexed, Allie stared up at Josh. "I'm not being nosy, but what did he mean by reckless?"

He smiled down at her. In time, he would wipe away her preconceived notions about him.

"Okay, I'm being nosy," she admitted beneath his unwavering gaze. "Hotdogger is a skiing term for someone who's—"

"Daring," he finished for her, his gaze flicking from her eyes to her mouth. He realized that he liked surprising her, throwing her a curve and seeing her blue eyes widen slightly. "Adam and I used to belong to the ski patrol together. The resort is lining up an exhibition show for their opening."

"Wait a minute." She looked puzzled. "When?"

"Who knows? When the snow falls heavy enough to—"

She shook her head wildly. "No, that's not what I meant. When were you on the ski patrol?"

"When I lived here before. Adam's an old friend."

"You must be very good."

He rocked a hand. "So—so."

"Modest, Professor?"

"We'll have to talk sometime." His knuckles brushed her cheek. "Then you can decide for yourself."

Allie fought a fluttery sensation and watched him stroll toward the checkout counter. She couldn't have responded even if she'd wanted to. A nervous excitement slithered through her. With a light caress, he'd made her skin tingle. What was he doing to her? she wondered, feeling a disturbance as chaotic as the flu sweeping through her. She pressed a hand to her stomach to stop the butterflies from fluttering, but she couldn't do a blessed thing about the heat he'd aroused.

Because she rushed through the last aisle to finish shopping, she gave in to impulse and spent more money than she planned to. Shoving the cart away from the checkout counter, she grimaced at the two full grocery bags she'd have to carry up the stairs.

Steps from the exit, she stopped and frowned as she noticed the miniature-size, stuffed animal sticking out of one of the grocery bags. Someone's child was going to be heartbroken. Allie did an about-face, hoping to find the child that the stuffed animal belonged to. "Adam." She held up the cuddly lion. "This isn't mine. You must have packed it in my bag by mistake."

He shrugged innocently at her. "It's yours."

Allie shook her head. "No, I didn't buy this."

"It's yours," he declared, grinning.

A realization slowly weaved its way to her. Josh? she mouthed.

Adam beamed back at her.

Her heart pitter-pattered. There was no other way to describe the slight skip, but she refused to blush. Yet, as she stepped out into the brisk autumn air, she felt the heat of a glow in her face. Damn. Each time they met, Josh confused her more.

By the time she reached home, her nerves hadn't calmed. He made her feel too much. For years, she'd kept a comfortable distance from others. When she'd left home after her breakup from Kyle, she'd faced facts. To win her family's approval, she would eventually have to end up like them—tied to a marriage that was filled with empty promises and bound to a job that demanded sacrificing everything else. She'd vowed to avoid them then, and now. Any involvement with Josh would threaten all she wanted—a life free and uncomplicated.

Struggling, she cradled a grocery bag in each arm, and contemplated with dread the number of climbs up the stairs before she would have carted all the pumpkins into her kitchen.

As she approached the outside stairs of the apartment building, she realized that all her resolve would be tested. Leaning against the banister, Josh was waiting for her as if it were expected. The collar of his jacket high on his neck, his hands stuffed in the pockets, he looked more like some roughneck seafaring type itching for a fight than academia personified.

Before she could protest, he slipped the grocery bags from her arms and started up the stairs. She trailed two steps behind him, her curiosity still more piqued about him than she wanted to admit. "Thank you for the lion, but why did you buy it?"

His pace continued steadily up the stairs. "Did it please you?"

"Yes, of course, but why—"

A slow smile lit his face. "To please you."

Allie frowned at his long legs. She rushed to catch up with him. "About what Adam said," she started. "Were you a member of the ski patrol when you were here before teaching?"

"No, I belonged when I was going to college here."

She scooted around him to block his path to her door. "You went to college here?"

"Why all the questions?"

Allie caught the hint of amusement in his voice. To say she was interested would be her downfall. "You don't look like the daredevil type."

"What type is that?"

As he sidestepped her and continued toward the door, she looked down to hunt for her keys in her purse. "Someone who thrives on excitement. Sky dives—"

"Yep."

Her head snapped up. In amazement she stared at him dumbly, but she'd never been at a loss for words for long. "River rafting?" she asked, slightly hesitant.

He nodded.

"Mountain climbing?"

He merely smiled.

Had she really believed that he had no sense of adventure? she wondered as she stepped ahead of him into the apartment. "They why? Why would someone who's done so much settle for this quiet existence?"

Following her to the kitchen, he responded easily. "This is what I've never done." While he transferred the bags onto the kitchen counter, he noticed that she'd shifted, relaxing and moving closer. At her questioning look, he explained. "My father was a musician. We bounced around from one city to the next. We rarely lived anywhere more than a few months, because he had jobs at local clubs all over the country. One of them was in Barrington. It was a place where they wanted the big band sound. He had the job until the owners realized that they'd better cater to the college students or close the doors. But we were here nearly a year. That was longer than we'd ever been anywhere else. I'd even begun to believe that we'd stay." He looked into one of the bags and stifled a smile at the sight of chocolate-covered marshmallow cookies. "I met Adam and other people then," he went on. "This town isn't too big," he added on a smile. "I hated leaving here."

She shrugged off her jacket and tossed it onto the closest chair. "So you decided to go to college here?"

"I promised myself I would. As a kid, I attended half a dozen schools," he said, digging in to unpack a bag. "The faces of hundreds of kids flash through my mind. I went my way. They went theirs. If I met any of them today and said my name, I bet that none of them would remember me. I was like the bird who nested in their tree one spring and never came back. No memory remains of me," he said simply. "Why should there be? I might remember a few names but no one who I'd call a friend."

Allie glanced up from unpacking the other bag. Facing her, he unzipped his jacket. Despite what he'd said about his unsettled past, he stood before her, looking rock-solid while her legs felt shaky.

"Most of my college friendships didn't last. I was limited in time because I had to work my way through."

"Your parents couldn't help?" she asked, thinking about her sisters' schooling. Law and medical schools had been paid for by her parents.

Thoughtfully he stared at her while she set the milk carton into the refrigerator. "My father never had steady work."

She leaned back against the refrigerator. "So you didn't go to Wainwright?"

He sent her a wry grin. "No, Wainwright means money. I went to the state university. But I lived in Barrington and commuted. I promised myself that I'd come back here. Every time I passed Wainwright, I made that promise to myself. After I graduated, I was offered a teaching job in Amherst. Eventually I earned my doctorate, and I applied for a position here."

Setting her palms on the counter, she hefted herself on it and leaned back against the cabinets. "And so here you are?"

"Nothing is that simple. It never has been. They needed a substitute when Professor Humboldt had his bypass operation. I took a chance and left my teaching position at the University of Massachusetts." He paused, remembering how uncertain he'd been about that decision. "The next semester Humboldt was back, and I was out hunting for a job. I taught at Syracuse until Wainwright offered me this position." He reached around her to set a can of peaches on the counter. In a tiny show of nerves, she leaned away to give him plenty of room.

"Where are your parents now?" Allie asked softly.

"My father died doing what he liked best. Playing the saxophone. He was working in a smoky dive. He'd been warned. The hours were wrong for a man with a heart condition. But he didn't care. He was a midnight man." He grabbed an empty garbage bag and folded it as he went on, "We were living in New Orleans then. He was playing the blues when his heart stopped. Neither my mother nor I were surprised. We knew it was a matter of time."

"How old were you?"

"Sixteen. The years after that weren't easy. He left my mother with nothing. So she went home again to New Bedford. In fifteen years, it was the first time she'd returned to the place where she'd been born. That's where she is now."

"Doing what?"

Affection slipped into his voice. "Finally making a home for herself. She had a promising career as a violinist but auditioning for the orchestra wasn't really possible anymore. Because we moved around so much, she couldn't dedicate herself to her music. While I was growing up, she took all kinds of jobs to pay the bills. Now, she claims that she's doing what she likes. She's teaching music at a private girls' school and has her own clientele. I'm not sure if she has regrets," he said more to himself than her.

"You never asked if she was unhappy?"

He raised his eyes to meet hers. Whether she realized it or not, she had a special talent—she knew how to listen for words not spoken. "No," he admitted. He looked away, uncomfortable with his own thoughts. "I couldn't talk to her about him. She loved him. It was that simple for her. But she sacrificed a lot for him. I realized that my father loved her in his own way. He was a good man," he said softly. "He was just lousy as a supporter. He shouldn't have gotten married or had a family." He shrugged one shoulder. "I never understood why he didn't want to give her more."

Allie inclined her head questioningly.

"She never said too much," he explained, "but her mother, my grandmother, told me at my father's funeral that she was supposed to audition for the Boston Philharmonic. Days before the audition, my father had an offer for a job—his big chance. It was in Chicago. Instead of auditioning, my mother went with him. She gave up a lot." He paused for a long moment. "I think that she gave up the star within her grasp for the one he never had any chance of catching." He met her gaze and saw the faint crease between her fair brows. "Why the frown?"

"I think you're very serious about everything."

"Serious?"

"Even a little narrow minded."

His head snapped up. For the briefest of seconds, a glint of annoyance darkened his eyes, but if her comment stirred his anger, he hid it well. "Why would you say that?" he asked in a voice so incredibly quiet that it seemed more unnerving than if he'd yelled.

"Maybe, she never wanted it." The look of puzzlement in his eyes assured her that he'd never considered such a thing. "But you assume—" Her words trailed off as he closed the distance between them. Allie fought the tensing of her body, the lightning quick thrill sweeping through her as his breath warmed her cheek.

He brushed a corner of her lips with his fingertips then strayed to her jaw. "Why do you do that?"

"Do what?" she asked almost warily.

"Deliberately try to irritate me."

She shook her head. "I wasn't—"

He felt her draw a quick breath. "It doesn't work," he said with deliberate softness, his eyes once again on her lips. "Anger isn't the emotion I feel when I'm with you," he whispered.

The softness in his voice swirled around her like a warm caress. She held her breath, unable to move as his mouth hovered close to hers, and she anticipated another kiss. To her surprise, he turned away without another word and strode out the door.

She'd underestimated him. Reckless didn't go hand-in-hand with staid. And conservative men didn't make a woman's heart pound and adrenaline pump. So who was he? One moment he epitomized everything she'd left behind her when she'd moved out of her parents' home. The next moment he seemed to be nothing like anyone she'd ever known. An enigma, Allie decided, wishing she didn't find him quite so intriguing.

As if she'd run a marathon, her heart refused to slow down. She pressed a hand to her chest, wishing she wouldn't react so easily to him. But he excited her. And she was such a sucker for excitement, she thought worriedly.

She finished folding the garbage bags. As she jammed the last one in the cupboard, she heard the click of her door opening.

He strolled in with a half-dozen pumpkins in his arms. "I figured you'd need someone to help haul these up."

"Thanks," she said weakly, concerned she wouldn't manage even a minute more with him without that excitement weakening her. As he carefully set the pumpkins on the kitchen counter, she searched for some simple way to make him rush from her apartment. "I really appreciate your volunteering to help carve them."

At her door, he swung a look back over his shoulder at her. "Carve?"

Allie grinned widely, certain Professor Josh MacKenzie wouldn't waste his time doing an activity indulged in by children under ten, parents and young-at-heart adults. He was definitely not the whimsical type.

She was wrong.

Three hours later, she was forced to admit that he was a good sport. As he notched out the jagged, uneven teeth on the twelfth pumpkin, Allie tilted her head speculatively. "You already made a triangle nose on the last three pumpkins."

"So?" he countered while wiping a paper towel over slippery fingers.

"So, the children will wonder if these came off an assembly line."

"No, they won't," he said with a hint of annoyance while shaking his head. "See that one," he said, pointing. "It's different from the one next to it."

They looked alike to her. "No, they're not."

"Sure, they are. That one," he said, jabbing a finger in the direction of the pumpkin, "has pointed brows. The other one has curved."

Allie took a step back and raised a hand as if measuring the quality of some masterpiece. "Yes, I see that now,'' she gibed, making sure he saw her roll her eyes.

''No appreciation,'' he grumbled.

''I appreciate your help,'' she said honestly and strode to the counter to line up the pumpkins. ''I hadn't expected it.'' She heard the scrape of his chair as he pushed it back. Thinking he was leaving, she whirled around.

He stood practically on top of her. As he placed a palm on each side of her, Allie was trapped by more than his body. He drew fantasies to a woman's brain. Strong, intelligent, handsome men possessed lethal weapons against a woman's resistance.

''Weren't you ever taught not to stereotype people?'' he asked quietly. ''You don't know me. And I don't know you.''

''No, we don't know each other,'' Allie said on a rushed breath as he lightly rested his fingers on the small of her back. ''But it's obvious that we have nothing in common.''

''You sound certain of that.''

''I am. We don't like to do the same things.''

''Like what?''

She searched for something that she didn't think he'd perfected. ''Bowl? Do you like to bowl?'' Because he hesitated, she jumped in quickly, ''See you don't.''

''When?''

The heat of his breath flowed across her face with that one word. Leaning back slightly, she parroted, ''When?''

''When do you want to go?''

Never if possible, she wanted to say. She was a terrible bowler. Slowly he grinned as if he'd read her mind.

"Why not right now?" he insisted.

Chapter Six

Laughingly she rolled her tenth gutter ball. He had to know she'd only pretended a love for the sport, but he was gentleman enough not to mention it.

He also refrained from comment the next day while they rode bikes up and down the streets. Her leg muscles said plenty. They quivered in complaint for four hours after. But she couldn't remember a time when she'd enjoyed herself more.

That worried her. No, it terrified her. She didn't want to become involved with him. Passion could be ignored or satiated. But what would she do about the way he made her feel? How would she ignore the longing for the sight of him? Certain she was becoming her own worst enemy, she relied on his good sense to stop them from getting further involved. Because she sensed his disapproval of the BBG's plans to spruce up the garbage cans, she bought two cans of red paint and deliberately set them outside her apartment door the next morning. He would view her plans as ridiculous. He would acknowledge how wrong they were for each other, and he would back off, she decided.

Josh saw the paint before he left for work. He gave her intentions only a cursory thought, but while driving, he caught himself glancing down alleys and looking for red garbage cans.

She wasn't easy to understand, but she also wasn't a woman who wouldn't be liked. He enjoyed being with her. He'd had fun with her, and he wanted her. He wanted her more than he'd wanted any woman in his life. But something more complex than desire drew him to her. Yet, to say he had no doubts would have been foolish.

At noon, he strode toward the refectory, wondering if she was sleeping now, wondering if two people living such opposite life-styles could find time for each other.

At the quick click of footsteps behind him, Josh swung a glance back over his shoulder.

A briefcase dangling from his hand, Nate approached at a clipped pace. "Where are you going?"

Josh waited at the entrance of the building. "Lunch."

Nate caught his arm. "Are you forgetting your lunch date with Carol?"

Josh frowned. Carol? Who the hell was Carol? He gave his head a mental shake before he remembered agreeing to meet another of Nate's "perfect women."

As Josh grimaced, Nate laughed. "You must have something important on your mind to forget a date with a lovely lady. This could be the one," Nate added.

Josh doubted that. The right one seemed to be the wrong one.

"Don't forget the college is supposed to be represented at tomorrow's festivities in the town square. If nothing else, the food is always good at the Founder's Day picnic," Nate quipped before turning away.

Josh's forced smile faded. How could he have forgotten the lunch date? He prided himself on his memory. His ability for remembering had led him to teach history. Dates, places, names never left his mind. But he'd forgotten a simple lunch date. Why was easy to answer. Thoughts of Allie filled his mind.

He would meet the woman for lunch. He would give his best effort to enjoy her company, but he sensed that he'd be fighting himself. One woman haunted him. He didn't want to be with anyone but her.

Allie dodged Josh for a full day. One long day and night, she mused, as she signed off and handed the microphone over to Kirby Delmont, KFKQ's morning man.

As she strolled out of the room, she was greeted by the first hint of sunrise. It peeked through a blind and cast a soft light into the hallway.

With a cup in her hand, one of the switchboard operators smiled from feet away. "Morning, Allie."

Running a hand across tight neck muscles, Allie returned a smile.

"What time are you doing the live broadcast today?"

"Nine to midnight."

The woman feigned a shiver. "It'll be cold."

"I doubt if I'll have more than a dozen brave souls out there with me. Along with the resident town square owl and a couple of policemen."

"Why doesn't the town hold this annual shindig earlier in the year?"

"Because Barrington wasn't founded until late October," Allie reminded her.

"Oh, yeah, that's right. Well, I'll see you there later."

"It'll be nice to see a familiar face."

"All of KFKQ will be there. Mr. Clements sent down a directive. Everyone is to show up and help promote the station." She cast a quick glance around her and then lowered her voice. "Did you hear the latest gossip from yesterday?"

Allie gave her a bland look, not interested in knowing which secretary Junior was chasing around a desk this week.

"I heard that B.J. is going to axe Junior."

Allie paid more attention.

"Want his job?"

Allie shook her head. "They'll probably offer the program director's position to someone outside of KFKQ."

"That's what Neil said."

The woman had practically swooned from the first moment that she'd seen Neil. Allie couldn't recall one conversation with her when Neil's name hadn't been mentioned.

"Neil said that some idiot from outside who knows nothing will probably get it."

Allie shrugged. "Neil's probably right."

The woman's face brightened. "Oh, I'm sure he is. He's so confident, so smart. So perfect."

Allie watched her stroll away. The woman was viewing Neil through rose-colored glasses. Neil wasn't dumb, but he was a little too cocky, and he definitely wasn't perfect. Allie had never felt any attraction for him. Too bad. Like her, he believed in no strings. They needed freedom, excitement. Whenever she stayed too long in any place, she felt closed-in. Neil understood. They were two of a kind.

Only he wasn't the one who ignited sparks within her when he touched her. That she needed to show good sense amused her. How many times during her childhood had she been chided for lacking it?

"Tired?"

Jarred from her thoughts, Allie jumped and wheeled around.

Chad gave her a crooked grin. "Sorry."

"That's okay." Allie managed a smile while her heart thudded against the wall of her chest. "I'm a little skittish. I didn't expect anyone but Kirby and Lynn to be here. It's kind of early for you to be here, isn't it?"

With his wide grin, the sparse mustache that he'd started growing twitched upward at one corner. "I'm working overtime for extra money." His smile faded. "You shouldn't be alone here so much. It isn't safe for a woman."

She managed a smile, hoping to make light of the discussion as much for herself as him. "The doors are all locked at night. And when Neil leaves, he double-checks them." Though Chad was innocent enough, something about him unnerved her. When a stranger stood too close in an elevator, he invaded what was known as a "comfort zone." Chad always seemed to be invading hers.

"I'll see you later today, won't I?" he asked.

Allie frowned. "Later?"

"Aren't you going to the picnic?"

"Maybe. It depends on how much sleep I get." She took a hesitant step then squeezed between him and the wall to reach the doorway. With a glance back, she noticed his eyes were still on her. Before she'd thought him shy. Neil considered him a creep. Whatever Chad's problem was, Allie wished he would solve it soon.

She didn't consider herself paranoid, but ever since her secret admirer had sent her his sick token of admiration, she'd gotten edgy. Even while broadcasting, she caught herself constantly glancing around, squinting at shadows and jumping at the slightest noise.

Though the nervousness slithered away after several hours, she only felt safe when she was home. Ironically she'd begun to realize that Josh being near was part of the reason.

She strolled toward the exit, wondering how she had always dodged such feelings before for a man. What formula had she used to be so successful at keeping her life free of emotional involvement? Men she'd known in the past who weren't as intent on keeping their freedom as she was usually ran. The moment she'd done anything that hadn't complied to conventional accepted behavior, they'd backed away. Why wasn't Josh? And why for a predictable man, did he keep sliding out of character even in the most minor but annoying ways?

"Allie, wait a minute."

A masculine hand reached forward to open the door for her. Tension rippled through her as she met Sam Bailey's eyes. It was their first one-on-one meeting since she'd taken over his time slot. "How are you?"

"I'm fine," he said with an edge of sarcasm. He looked down, gesturing at the carton cradled in his arm. "I came to do a final cleaning out of my desk."

Allie waited for him to open the door and then preceded him outside. Though the wind whipped at her, she found his tone more cutting. Raising her collar almost protectively, she asked the obvious question. "Have you found another job?"

"I found one," he responded curtly. A tiredness suddenly settled over his face and he looked away. On a heavy sigh, he faced her. "Sorry. This isn't your fault."

"I'm sorry, too. I thought you were good for this station."

"I was," he said with a confidence that deejays were forced to develop as protection. Tough hides were a necessity in their occupation.

"Where are you going?" Allie asked.

"Some little town in South Dakota. Maybe, they'll think I'm the greatest thing since the carving of Mount Rushmore."

Knowing he was attempting to lighten the mood, Allie cooperated. "They will." She touched his arm. "Good luck, Sam."

"Thanks." He started to turn away then stopped. "Do you have a contract?"

"I didn't want one," she admitted.

"Geez, Allie, that's gutsy."

"I don't want to be bound to this station."

"Probably just as well. Don't get too comfortable with the job. The ax falls swiftly."

"I've experienced it before."

His lips twisted in a semblance of a smile. "We all have. Take care."

"You, too," she said before turning toward the parking lot. She was one of the lucky ones, she decided not for the first time. She had no family to support so she didn't need the security of a job. She had no grand illusions of being "the one and only" on the air so she felt no disappointments when she was forced to leave by management's decree. She had choices. Few people had such freedom.

Her head bent, Allie dug into her purse and hunted for her keys. At five in the morning, a quietness prevailed that allowed her to hear the slightest sound—the bang of a door, the caw of a crow, the whistle of the wind. What she rarely heard were another person's footsteps. As someone's clicked in duet with hers, she glanced around her. Though she saw no one, her heart quickened. She wouldn't spook herself. So she'd received dead flowers and a few mysterious phone calls. Barrington was small. Quiet. It was a peaceful town where the biggest crime was some prank performed by the college students.

She took a few deep, relaxing breaths. When had she become so jumpy? She had to forget the pranks that were making her afraid of her own shadow. She'd fought too hard for independence, to give up so easily.

She hurried toward her car. At the sight of Bill Vannen Jr., the station owner's son, she steeled herself to his inevitable lascivious comment. Though he wasn't her favorite person, she was relieved at having an explanation for the footsteps she'd heard.

He flashed a broad grin at her. "Hi, pretty Allie."

"Hi, Junior. What are you doing here so early?"

"I dropped in to see if the programming schedule was up."

"Dropped in?" she asked, remembering the hours that his predecessor had spent at the radio station.

He shrugged a beefy shoulder. "You know, Allie, I could show you a really good—"

"She's busy."

Junior's head swiveled as if tugged by a puppeteer's string.

Leaning against the door of her Mustang, Josh said no more. Nothing was needed. His stance was firm, combative.

Junior swayed back from her. "I heard you weren't seeing anyone."

"You heard wrong," Josh cut in, approaching them.

Junior grunted. "You'll never know what you missed, Allie." Though his tone was egotistical, Allie noted that he hurried away before Josh reached them.

Josh had taken a chance. Fierce jealousy knotted his stomach while he'd watched the man leering at her. He couldn't believe she would be interested in the smooth lines of some ex-football moron. "Did you mind?" he asked, slipping a proprietorial hand over Allie's arm.

"Actually, I owe you a favor," she said lightly.

Her pleased look moved him. He'd awakened tired, thinking about her *again*, needing to see her. "Good. Then have breakfast with me," he requested, touching the small of her back and urging her toward the car.

As she turned toward it, she saw the picnic basket on the hood. "What's that for?"

"A sunrise picnic. Breakfast. Or dinner," he added quickly, grinning at her.

A laugh tickled her throat that this man who believed in a definite order of things would suggest a sunrise picnic. "What's in the basket really? Twinkies?"

He gently touched her arm. "Something that resembles brown grass?"

Allie fought the wind chilling her and lifted one side of the basket to peek in. Wrapped in plastic was a plate of bite-size melon slices and red juicy strawberries. "You're serious?"

"As you told me, I'm always serious." He waited until her eyes met his. Eyes that were soft and understanding, impish and smiling, eyes that he could look at forever and never tire of. "And being with you seemed like a nice way to start the day."

Her heart fluttered. She couldn't believe it. The last time her heart fluttered she'd been sixteen and gaga over the captain of the football team. If only he'd act insufferable, dignified and disapproving, then she would feel safer. If he'd stop doing unexpected, surprising things, she could remember why she should stay clear of him. But he kept showing her sides of him that she didn't want to see, the part of him that could weaken her. "What else is in there besides fruit and alfalfa sprouts?" she asked before tapping a finger at the basket.

"Wait and see." The basket in one hand, he slipped his fingers beneath her elbow and urged her toward his car.

Allie balked and looked back. "What about my car?"

"I'll drive you back here for it. Let's take mine. I need to stop at one store, though." As the wind tossed her hair, he released her arm and raised his hand to brush strands away from her cheek. "But I made sure that I brought pickles."

On a laugh, she slid into his car. "How can I resist."

They drove along a country road lined with trees painted crimson and gold. Tied to the antenna of Josh's car and bobbing in the air was the bright cherry-red balloon she'd bought at the store for him. Josh knew he would get plenty of stares when he drove into the faculty parking lot with that balloon, but he didn't care. The balloon would stay until the last breath of air within it died.

"I've always loved the scenery here," Allie said as she stared out the window at a sky gray with a hint of sunlight. "Do you know that geologists believe that the mountains in this area haven't changed in millions of years. I always find that amazing." She swiveled a glance at him. "What Indian tribe settled this area?"

He started to answer, but seeing the slip of a smile curling her lips, he felt a laugh stirring within him. "Is this a quiz?"

She held two fingers closely together. "A little one."

"Do you know?" Josh asked and then waited.

"Algonquins," she responded.

He nodded and returned his attention to the bumpy road. "How do you know the history?"

She stretched on the seat beside him. "I make it a point to learn everything I can about everywhere I go."

Puzzled, Josh frowned. She wanted no roots, yet she deliberately gave herself memories. His mother always had, too. She'd told him once that the more comfortable she was with a place, the easier it was to think of it as home. He said nothing, but he found the remark more revealing than Allie might realize.

By the time they'd spread a blanket on a patch of grass sheltered by oaks, the sun was firmly peeking at the horizon. Enthusiastically Allie dug into the picnic basket beside her. "You bought fried chicken?"

"After seeing what you had in your grocery cart, I wasn't sure if you'd eat it."

As she took a hearty bite of a chicken leg, he grinned slowly in a way that was becoming too familiar to her. She shook her head while she dabbed the napkin at her mouth. "I love fried chicken, barbecue ribs, pizza, anything messy, anything that I can eat with my fingers. I only eat health foods when I gain weight."

Carefully, he poured coffee from a thermos into a cup. With her reed-thin shape, he wondered if such a thing were possible.

"You see, I lied." Her nose wrinkled with her wide grin.

"Lied about what?"

"This," she said, setting a box of gooey-looking, chocolate-glazed doughnuts on the blanket. "When we stopped at the store, I bought these. They're for you."

He laughed. "And you?"

"Thank you for offering," she said without a hint of hesitation and reached into the box for one.

He grimaced as she took a bite of a strawberry then a pickle and then the chocolate doughnut. "You must have a cast iron stomach."

"It's not overly sensitive," she assured him while picking up a slice of melon. Though the conversation had been light, Allie felt as if nerves were strung tight. She wasn't a nervous person by nature. But she realized that she needed every moment with him consumed by conversation. Silences unsettled her. Silences made her remember his kisses and the sensations he'd aroused. "I never thanked you for coming to my defense back at the radio station." While the faint heat of the morning sun caressed her back, a chilling breeze curled around her. "Junior isn't any real threat," she went on, "but he is annoying."

"Cold?" he asked, noting her shiver and reaching around her to raise the collar of her jacket. He watched the wind ruffle her hair. Sunlight danced across strands of it, highlighting gold threads. He wondered why any man would seek a more superficial treasure than a woman who brought sunshine into his life. "You need a little looking after," he said softly.

Allie forced herself to meet his eyes. Beneath the grayness of morning still mantling them, his looked darker. "I've been on my own for a while."

"Did you ever want to do anything else?"

Drawing back, she tipped her head questioningly. "Did you? Were you a typical boy, wanting to be a baseball player when you grew up?"

"No." He traced a fingertip lightly across the line of her jaw. "I wanted to be a world-renowned physicist."

A shiver slithered across her flesh. "I should have known."

He laughed softly. "I was like every other kid. I wanted to be another Babe Ruth."

"But you gave up that goal?"

"We moved around so much that I never had time to belong to any team. So I reconsidered and chose a more practical profession."

"I wanted to be the first woman in space."

"And gave it up?" he asked.

"Modified it," she said, relaxing slightly as he leaned back. "Now, I want to be the first person to communicate with an extraterrestrial." While she'd responded with a lighthearted remark, he arched a brow as if seriously considering what she'd said.

"That could be possible."

She squinted at him for a long moment. "Why didn't you tell me that what I want is silly?"

He took a long drink of coffee. "It isn't. It's possible."

Allie sighed. "You're not supposed to respond that way."

He chuckled at the annoyed look on her face. "What should I have said?"

"Something suitable. My sister, Marilyn, would have told me that I'm inclined to be a little spacey anyway. But then she never swiped cookies, either."

With a few revealing words, she snagged more than his interest. He rested back against a tree trunk and waited, hoping to understand her better.

"The cook always made spice cookies on Wednesdays," she explained. "Sarah, my other sister, and I would sneak into the kitchen and take cookies. But not Marilyn. Oh, no. Honest Hannah wouldn't think of doing that."

On a laugh, he slid his hand over hers that was resting on the blanket.

Allie felt herself responding to that accepting touch. Because he seemed to understand that along with sibling rivalry was love, she spoke freely. "She must have been destined to be on the side of justice even then, but I always wondered how someone quite so honest in so many ways could be so dishonest to herself."

"In what way?"

"My sister wanted a position at a prestigious law firm and so conveniently she met and married a district court judge's son."

Though not a blind idealist, Josh never considered marrying for position. In some ways, he and Allie were more alike than she realized.

Seeing his frown, she added, "It isn't as bad as it sounds. My family has a very pragmatic view about marriage. My mother wouldn't divorce my father until last year even though the marriage fell apart a decade ago."

A frown veed his brows. "Why not?"

"She wanted to win votes. First for the city council then the mayoralty. When she finally agreed to the divorce, my father admitted to all of us that he'd married her because his father had offered money for a research project he was working on if he settled down."

Was that part of the problem between them? Josh wondered. Did she think he was like them? Calculating, emotionless to everything but success. The idea angered him. He'd never used or hurt anyone to get where he was. "Wasn't there anyone in your family who married for the real reason?"

She waited, wanting him to say the one word.

"Love?" he asked with her continued silence.

"Love eludes anyone named Gentry," she said too lightly. "No, that's not really true." She smiled with a warm memory. "My grandfather loved all of us, not caring what our faults were." Humor edged her voice. "Probably because he was the family eccentric. On any given day, we never knew what he'd do next. Sometimes I'd find him in the kitchen baking bread or he'd be outside feeding birds. He drove everyone crazy," she said laughingly. "Like I said, he was the family crackpot. He told me that he'd will me that title when he died." She expected him to give her an exasperated shake of his head. Instead, he smiled, the hand on hers tightening. Against her will, her heart softened. "But his marriage to my grandmother was for financial gain on her part. He and my grandmother were divorced before I was born. Everyone has been divorced at least once."

For someone whose parents weathered the bad with the good for seventeen years, Josh didn't understand such lack of commitment. Idealistic or not, to him, marriage was forever. "And the ex-fiancé? What about him?"

Her smile faded swiftly as she recalled some of the worst days in her life. "He loved to suffocate me. It was my own fault," she admitted. "I shouldn't have gotten involved with Kyle. But I knew it was what everyone expected. It was my one chance to do something everyone would approve of."

"And that was important?"

She huddled deeper in her jacket, needing some barrier from him. He probed too much, his questions always making her say more than she'd intended. "Then. Not now. When I was younger, I deliberately did things to make waves around the house. One summer I cultivated a night and day enjoyment of country and western music. The following spring, I was determined to get a black belt in karate. My family disapproved of both things. But what I started as adolescent rebellion, I soon began to enjoy." Her eyes brightened with a smile. "I'm sure that they had private talks often, wondering where I fit in. And," she said on a lighter note, "they couldn't pretend I was adopted." She wrinkled her nose to stir his smile. "I have my mother's nose."

Cute nose, he thought.

"And my father's eyes and hair."

He stared at the blond hair that reminded him of wheat swaying beneath the brightness of the sun.

She saw a warmth in his eyes that had nothing to do with passion, and she found it more unsettling than any of the others. She needed to end this. She had to do it now or she might not be able to later. And in the end, they would both be hurt. For the end would come. Soon, perhaps, she thought, deciding to share some news with him. "I might be leaving soon," she said a little too abruptly to sound as matter-of-fact as she'd hoped.

Josh managed to hide his own displeasure. "New job?"

"Yes, and I'm looking forward to it." Oddly she had to feign enthusiasm. "Neil heard about an exciting opportunity in Los Angeles for a morning show. We might apply as a team," she added, but acknowledged that until that moment she hadn't seriously considered the idea. Nice as Neil was, he was also a big talker. Unless someone from Los Angeles phoned and personally talked to her, she would continue to doubt that the deal existed.

"But it isn't definite?"

The eyes on her were steady, like the man. "No, it's not definite," she answered honestly. "I always enjoy new places though. New surroundings. New people. I move because I'd be bored living in the same place all the time."

"Why?" He couldn't veil his confusion and damned himself for letting it show. "One place doesn't have to be boring. If it's special. Just as one woman won't be boring," he said softly. "If she's special."

Part of her wanted to take his words to heart.

"You are," he said with certainty.

In a second, he made her blood pound, swayed her, she realized as she caught herself leaning closer to him. She let out a deep breath and rushed to gather her plate and fork and set them back into the basket. "I enjoyed the picnic. The strawberries were good and—" Words remained unsaid as he closed his hand over her wrist, keeping her from drawing back. "The strawberries were good," she muttered inanely again.

"I know something sweeter."

Her pulse scrambled as he caught her chin and held her face still with a touch that was so light she barely felt it. "We don't view life through the same window," she insisted but closed her eyes as he lightly caressed her eyelids with his mouth.

"Kind of philosophical."

Allie stilled as he slid his hand behind her neck and his lips nipped at the corner of hers. "But true."

"Not always."

She wanted to run from what she couldn't deny.

"You bought the balloon, and I left it on my car."

"But it won't stay on." Beneath the touch of his lips on her cheekbone, she felt his smile. "It'll drift away," she insisted.

Like she would, he reminded himself. The thought was one that he didn't want to consider at the moment. "It'll stay for as long as it was meant to stay."

She wasn't immune to his charm. Her lashes fluttered as his mouth touched a vulnerable spot near her ear. "There'll never be anything more between us," she said as firmly as she could on a sigh.

While he'd counted on politeness to back her into a corner, he wondered how she could even utter the ridiculous words. From the beginning, it had been clear to him that there would be much more between them. "You believe people can switch feelings on and off, don't you?" he whispered before pressing his lips against hers in caress of a kiss.

"I don't know." Her pulse quickened, mocking her. "But I'm trying," she managed huskily as the taste of him lingered on her lips. "I'm attracted to you. But we don't want the same things." She steadied her breathing. "We're too different."

"You can't simplify this."

"This is simple."

"I wish it was," he said softly, more to himself than her. How easy it would be if all that mattered was sex. But more than desire led him, magnetized him to her.

As he tangled his fingers in her hair and brushed her mouth with his, lightly at first as if testing, a jolt charged through her. Without hesitation, her lips parted in response to the deepening pressure of his kiss. She couldn't bring forward even the weakest protest.

Though she placed a hand against his shoulder, instead of pushing away, she melted against him. Her wrist went limp and then slowly she slid her fingers up to the back of his neck. Beneath her palm, she felt the warmth of his skin. A soft sigh escaped from her throat as his breath mingled with hers. His sweet, savoring play, the demanding firmness of his lips, the moist heat of his tongue insisted on her response. With a kiss, he was making every denial that she'd uttered sound like a lie. She felt his hand moving over her, his caress steady, confident as if he had a right to touch her softness.

A yearning gnawed at her, building with such speed that she felt fear rush through her. And as her heart raced and threatened to accompany the rising heat in her blood, she knew how close she was to letting all reasoning flee. If she didn't stop him, she would give in to everything he made her feel. Even as pleasure rippled through her, she wrenched her lips from his and steeled herself as much to her own feelings as his response.

"You know that we're already involved," he whispered, his mouth taunting hers. "I want you." Impatience threaded in his voice. "And you can keep denying it to yourself, but your kisses tell me that you want me, too."

Her heart thudded as if it would burst through her chest. She heard the usual softness in his voice, and she felt the tenderness in his touch, but his eyes were darker, intense with emotion. "You don't look like an impulsive man," she said on a whisper.

"Impulse? You think that was said impulsively? Hardly," he muttered, linking his hands with hers and drawing her to a stand with him. "I've thought about this long and hard."

His eyes locked with hers, pulling at her, urging her closer without a touch.

"Now, it's your turn."

Chapter Seven

Never had anyone disrupted her life in quite the same way. Needing something to occupy her mind, Allie rushed through a dozen household chores to keep busy that afternoon. She cleaned her apartment until it gleamed, baked five cakes and soaked in a relaxing bath, but nothing helped. By early evening, the cakes were being eaten at a nearby nursing home, and she began dressing for KFKQ's contribution to the Founder's Day celebration, but with an overactive imagination in high gear, she still felt the heat of his mouth on hers.

A garbage bag in her hand, she huddled deeper in her jacket as she stepped outside. Where would Josh be while she was freezing at the town square? Warm, snug, settled back and reading a book?

Cursing her evening shift, she strolled toward the alley. Feet from it, she froze in mid-stride. As a laugh tickled the back of her throat, Allie felt her resistance to him dwindling away to nothing. Next to the official ugly garbage can was another—a bright red can engulfed by a wide pink ribbon and a gigantic pink bow.

As a feeling of helplessness drifted over her while she walked to the town square, she grappled to be realistic. Where would time with him lead? Nowhere. She would leave. He would stay. He wanted commitments. She wanted no strings. She tried to remember that they didn't belong together.

Shivering against the chill of the early evening air, she strolled through the crowd gathered on the grass and periodically stopped to sign autographs. Vermont bore a hearty stock of people. Without a care about the weather, they'd gathered to enjoy the celebration.

Colorful balloons danced in the air above a banner that stretched from one tall oak to another. The Georgian structure of city hall, the park fountain and a grotesquely huge statue of Barrington's founder offered the backdrop to the small podium.

For a few moments, she watched the ferris wheel's circular motion. In the adjacent park, several men, including Josh, played baseball. He swung the bat and missed, but on the next pitch, he powed the ball out of the park. He played the game like a Class A jock, she thought resignedly. Brawn and brains only emphasized what she'd been trying to remember all along. He was one of the close to "perfect" people in the world. He was exactly the kind of man she'd sworn to stay clear of. But how could she ignore a man who'd painted a garbage can red for her, who'd offered a simple but reassuring squeeze of her hand when she'd talked about her family, who'd protectively run interference against Junior? Once intimacy linked them, that man wouldn't be easy to forget. Ever.

She had no answers for what she felt for him. She only knew that while she didn't want to be hurt, she couldn't disregard the emotions slithering through her whenever she was near him.

Her own ambivalence worried her. On a heavy sigh, she ambled past concession stands where homemade jellies and breads and cakes were being sold. Restless from her own thoughts, she stood indecisively for a long moment before she oriented herself and set off in a definite direction.

Near the podium, Neil finished scribbling his name on a sheet of paper for a dreamy-eyed teenager. Though he sent her a knock-the-socks-off smile, his attention shifted to Allie. "What are you doing here so early?"

"I came to enjoy myself for a few hours." She pointed to a booth where a game of chance was being offered. "Did you try that?"

"Nope." He glanced at the youth who was aiming a gun at cardboard ducks. "I have all the luck I need. I have great news, Allie baby. Great news," he said in an excited voice. "California is seriously considering us. They want us to send a demo to them on the double."

"On the double," she repeated, smiling at his excitement.

"Pronto."

"When do you want to do it?"

"I made arrangements."

"You are anxious, aren't you?"

He slid his arm around her shoulder. "You'll be, too, as soon as you hear the salary."

Allie was impressed.

"Stay Thursday morning and I'll come in so we can do the demo for them."

Allie nodded agreeably. Possibly Neil wouldn't have noticed. Whistling, he climbed the few steps onto the podium. She sensed that he saw his name, only his name, in lights. But neither money nor fame led her. She'd gone into broadcasting because it was fun. She liked people. And through the years, she'd learned that many of the listeners considered deejays their friends.

"Quite a crowd, huh?" Neil chirped from his platform.

Allie doubted that she would see half that number when she finished her airtime.

By midnight, as expected, she counted no more than eight people. Along with a few students who'd braved the night chill on a lark, her audience included the two policemen on duty, a stray cat or two and the town's resident park owl, affectionately referred to as Dr. Seuss.

Allie peered at her watch. She had two minutes more of airtime. For the special broadcast, she worked until midnight then continuous prerecorded music would begin from the radio station. She signed off then waited to hear the announcement of the station's call letters before she removed the bulbous earphones.

Josh lounged against a towering oak. While crime in Barrington was low, he couldn't stay home in a warm apartment while she was shivering in the cold. When she stepped from the podium, he pushed away from the tree.

"This is above the call of duty even for a member of Wainwright's faculty," a voice quipped behind him. As he swung around, Nate hunched his shoulders against the cold. "You didn't have to stay here all night. Why are you still here?"

"I could ask you the same thing," Josh returned, fixing his gaze on three men who were swaying their way around the rows of chairs in front of the podium. Decent men sometimes acted like fools. He'd traveled too much and seen enough drunks at the places where his father had played to last him a lifetime. When Allie started across the grass, they swaggered toward her. Josh couldn't decipher more than one of the men's slurred, "Hey, sweetie."

"I have insomnia," Nate said, cutting into Josh's thoughts. "Walking before bedtime helps. My wife says—"

As the one man grabbed Allie's arm, Josh tensed instinctively. With a quick step to the side, he brushed past Nate and then wound his way around rows of chairs to reach her. No more than seconds passed, but by the time he was within feet of her, Allie was already talking to the biggest man.

Beaming up at him, she looked unconcerned. "What's your name?"

He stared dumbfoundedly back at her as if his mind was too cloudy from drink to understand what was happening. "Earl," he finally managed.

"Well, Earl, if you give me the name of your favorite song, I'll make sure it's played tomorrow night at nine. And for coming out here so late at night, KFKQ has a special thank you."

Josh watched the man physically fold beneath her bright smile.

Handing him a card, Allie spoke softly, "This is for a free dinner for you and your favorite lady."

Josh knew who his favorite lady was. She had the bulky man docile and grinning.

Nate suddenly stood beside him again. "I want you to know," he said, winded from his race after Josh. "I was prepared to fight if you needed help."

Josh offered him a thank-you smile.

"Would have seemed like old times."

Aware Allie had control of the situation, Josh relaxed. "Were you pugnacious in your youth?"

Nate stretched himself straighter. "I was a Marine."

On a laugh, Josh touched his shoulder before closing the distance to meet Allie halfway. Protectively he slipped fingers around her arm. "You handled him well."

Even in the shadowed light, she could see the tension tightening his features. With a wave of her hand, she dismissed the notion that the three men were a threat. "They meant nothing, Josh. Too much liquor."

He knew that she was right, but worry for her plagued the tip of his thoughts constantly.

She shoved cold hands into the pockets of her jacket. "What are you doing out here so late?"

"Enjoying the weather."

An amused smile curved her lips before she looked up at the clouds drifting across the moon. "Do you have Eskimo blood in your veins?" she asked, visibly shivering.

He responded by draping an arm around her shoulder. "Actually it's rather warm these days."

Allie swayed against him, accepting the comfort of his body heat. "Is it?" she asked though she understood his words only too well.

He leaned closer and caressed strands of her hair. He was taunting himself, wanting to bury his face in their silky texture. "You know it is," he said softly, deciding talk might be his only defense against his preoccupation with her mouth, and the warm sweetness that her taste would bring him.

Allie had no response. Her senses ganged up on her when she was with him. Though the scent of approaching winter clung to the air, his aftershave was the only fragrance she smelled. While leaves rustled on the street, the softness of his voice lingered in her mind. And as the soft wail of the wind whistled through the trees, her own heart thundered from his nearness.

Her shoulders heaved as she took a calming breath. She needed conversation to keep traitorous thoughts at bay. "Twice you've come to my rescue," she said when they were climbing the stairs inside their building.

Shaking against a chill, Josh lowered the collar of his jacket. "I'd take a cup of coffee as a thank you."

The refusal on the tip of her tongue remained unsaid. As he froze beside her, she felt a shiver pass down her arms in response to the wreath of black carnations leaning against her apartment door.

Somehow, she stifled a gasp, but a numbing kind of fear slithered through her. Because it threatened to make her cling to him, she fought the thoughts accompanying it. Being in the public eye meant dealing with all kinds of people. "Do you think he left his calling card?"

Though she made the comment easily, Josh heard a trace of a tremble in her voice and moved forward ahead of her to retrieve the card attached to the wreath. When she joined him at the door, he reached for the small white envelope peeking out from the flowers. "Here," he said, handing it to her.

She tore open the envelope and read the scribbled signature. "Your secret admirer."

"Wonderful." Josh narrowed his eyes at the writing. "What about the handwriting? Do you recognize it?"

She shook her head and motioned toward the wreath before unlocking the door. "I'd rather not bring that in."

"I'll throw it in the garbage can for you while you put on the coffee." Without a word, he pushed past her to enter her apartment first.

With some amusement, she watched disbelief flash across his face after she opened the door. Frowning, he stepped over the pots and pans that she'd strung together and lined up in front of the door.

"What's this?" he asked with a downward gesture.

"A homemade burglar alarm," Allie said breezily, passing him quickly on legs not quite steady.

"You weren't worried at all, were you?" he quipped.

She waited while he played bloodhound through her apartment. "All clear?" she called out as he strode back into the living room.

"No goblins."

"Thank goodness. I never liked monster movies."

He noted that her eyes sparkled with private amusement as if she were determined not to let the memory of that wreath pull down her spirits. "Too scary?"

"No. But inevitably someone jumps out at the dummy who goes wandering in the house or the cave by herself. And I always lose a half box of popcorn on those scenes."

"Don't go alone," he said quietly. "Then someone with a stronger resistance to surprise can hold the popcorn for you."

"Like you, I suppose?"

"Like me." He visually circled the room. "Is everything all right here?"

"Everything is a mess."

The magazines on the sofa were the only disorder. As she snatched them up in a nervous rush, he couldn't humor her. He was becoming frightened for her. "You can't make light of what just happened," he insisted, determined to make her face the thread of danger that might coil around her if the person decided on more serious action.

She stopped in mid-stride, her hands falling to her sides. "What should I do?"

"Call the police."

"And tell them what?" she asked. "That someone is sending me flowers, but they're dead? If you were a detective, what would you say? Bad florist. Right?"

Looking away, he released an impatient breath. She was right. No threat had been made, but the underlying message was too clear for him to forget it.

"You know I'm right," she said, skirting him to head toward the kitchen.

"Allie, sit down."

"In a minute. Let me throw these magazines away first."

"We need—"

"These are my monthly reading requirements." At his puzzled frown, she forced a laugh as much for herself as him. "All of these magazines are from my sister Sarah. The doctor," she added as an explanation. "She feels compelled to send me articles to read. Articles about the unfulfilled woman, about biological clocks, about the psychological factors of living alone, about single people dying before married ones, about anything that she believes I need to read."

"Do you read them?"

"No," she responded without hesitation.

"It sounds as if she means well."

"She probably does. But I don't need tons of advice about how to live my life."

"Was that a subtle hint to me?" he asked, following her when she turned away. "Because if it was, I'm not paying attention. I don't give a damn what the police say. You should report this."

"I'm not listening." She dropped the magazines into a wastebasket.

In three strides, he caught up with her and grabbed her arm to stop her. "I'm a teacher. I'm used to talking to people who aren't listening to me."

She whirled toward him. "What does it matter who's playing this prank."

"Prank?"

"That's all it is."

"How do you know that?"

"Because no one has any reason to dislike me enough for me to take this seriously. And there's no real danger." She pushed away from him, and in passing, she flicked on the television set. "I always check to see if there's a good movie on when I come home." She removed the beige tam that had been precariously tilted on the left side of her head. "If there is, I make popcorn," she said, reaching up to pull the pins from her hair. "Would you like some?"

As her hair tumbled around her face, Josh recalled how soft the strands had felt beneath his fingers. On a silent curse, he whirled away, filled with more frustrations than he'd known in years. "Make the popcorn," he muttered as he opened the door. "I'll throw the wreath away. When I come back, I'll melt the butter."

Allie kicked off her shoes. He planned on melting something, but she suspiciously didn't think that something was butter.

As she rushed to the kitchen counter and began spooning coffee into the brewing basket, a sense of aloneness unlike any she'd ever known settled over her. She liked people around her, but she'd always been just as comfortable with solitude before—before she'd met him. Then, she'd been certain of what she wanted. Now, she wasn't sure of anything.

By the time he returned to her apartment, the aroma of the rich brew and the sound of popping corn filled the rooms. "It's almost done," she called out to him from the kitchen. With bowls of popcorn in her hands, she plopped on the sofa beside him.

Because she'd taken the trouble to make it, Josh accepted the bowl, but he was in no mood to eat the popcorn. A helplessness he'd never known before enveloped him. He'd never faced someone he cared about being threatened. He'd never felt the inkling of fear that if that person were out of his sight something might happen to her.

As if clutching for a lifeline, she forced a soft laugh while she struggled to forget the ominous wreath and the person who'd sent it. "I love any movie with Bogart, Garfield or Cagney," she mumbled before tossing popcorn in her mouth.

Draping an arm behind her on the sofa, he stared at the soundless screen, wondering if she planned on turning up the volume.

"Kyle used to—" She cut her words short, not believing how easily she'd started to confide in him.

"Kyle used to what?" he insisted.

"Prefer viewing x-rays. We bored each other silly."

Because she'd said it so matter-of-factly, he sensed that she'd been hurt more than she wanted anyone to know. Instinctively he closed a comforting hand over her shoulder. "Did you think the ex-fiancé might be the one and only?"

Her brows bunched with her frown as she held up her hand and counted off three fingers. "I've had three infatuations in which I was sure I'd die instantly if he *did* look at me. All before the age of sixteen," she added. "Then two iffys."

He smiled more at her effort to keep the moment light than at her words.

She leaned forward and set her popcorn bowl on the makeshift coffee table, a square box painted with blue and yellow strips. "There was a rock star—an electric guitarist with a punk hairstyle, skin-tight leather pants, and of course, poor hearing. And there was a nude model. The arty type. My parents didn't approve of either of them."

He understood why.

"Does that answer your question?"

Though she'd evaded answering his question, he held back from persisting. Instead his fingers linked with hers. "What happened to the ex?"

Allie sighed. He was going to force her to remember a time in her life that she'd nearly forgotten. No more pain, no more guilt weighed her down now. But at one time, she'd felt like such a failure. "He married someone like my sisters." As he leaned closer as if to see her face better, Allie resisted squirming. "I had the right name and the right background for a bound-for-success intern. But I lacked the tact to be the wife of a plastic surgeon. I wasn't honest with myself. He began paying attention to me and everyone in the family was thrilled. I guess that they believed I was finally going to do something normal."

He needed to reassure her. When they'd first met, he'd tagged her as an oddball. But what was so peculiar about anything she'd done? Brushing a strand of hair away from her cheek, he offered a weak smile. "You look normal to me."

"My family loves me," she assured him. "I know they do. But I can't be what they want me to be. I never will. And I couldn't be the perfectly groomed, well-mannered wife of a doctor. One night at a party of a highly respected plastic surgeon who was interested in an assistant, I aired my views on cosmetic surgery."

"Which is?"

She pointed down with her thumb. "By the time I was done, several women at the party were ready to tar and feather me. It seems that they were all clients of the well-known clay modeler."

His head went back with laughter.

"It really wasn't funny," she admonished but smiled.

"It's a great story though," he said, somewhat distracted as he toyed with a curl near her ear. He'd never met anyone like her before. He'd never known how quickly laughter could slip into any moment of his life.

"Why haven't *you* ever married?" she asked curiously.

He expected her disapproval but her honesty about her ex-fiancé forced him to reciprocate. "I had things to get done. I promised myself I'd do them first. I wouldn't put any woman through what my mother went through. I knew that I'd be selfish until I had my doctorate. It didn't seem fair."

Tucking her legs beneath her, she shifted toward him. "But what if you had met someone that—"

"I'd fallen in love with?" he finished for her while he traced the curve of her neck. Beneath his fingers, he felt none of the usual tenseness when he was so near. He burned with an ache for her. He'd spent months with other women and had never felt an inkling of what she'd aroused in him during such a short time. "I think I might be," he said softly.

Her eyes locked on his. Was she still breathing? she wondered. She couldn't take him seriously. Airily, she released a soft laugh. As he kissed the curve of her neck, she leaned away before he seduced her to the point where she couldn't think. "How does a person manage to keep this schedule?" Questions clung to her tone. "So many years set aside to go to school? So many years to establish yourself teaching? So many years to reach your goals? Is that how it goes?"

He drew a long breath, deciding that what had sounded so right to him for years had a ring of unpleasantness when she said it. "That's right." He sent her a wry grin. "To be honest with you, I figured that I might never find anyone. Until now."

Her chin raised as if someone had thrown a punch at it. "I was nearly married, Josh, and I'm the one who didn't make it work."

"Or the one brave enough to admit something was wrong."

She tilted her head. No one had ever said those words to her before. Desperately she'd wished for someone to understand when she'd broken off with Kyle, and no one had.

"You can't fail at something you never wanted to succeed at, Allie." He brought her hand to his mouth and lightly kissed her palm. "He didn't make you feel as if you couldn't stand a moment without him, did he?"

Heat swept from her hand upward. "No," she answered on a slow shake of her head.

"That's what you make me feel," he said softly, threading his fingers into her hair while he pressed his lips to the curve of her jaw.

As his tongue glided across her skin, sensation held her still. "This won't work." She attempted to protest but her body trembled with emotion as he directed his play to the sensitive flesh below her ear. "This is—"

"Wonderful," he murmured.

His voice was too soft, too compelling. Why with a few words did he freeze her to a spot? Instead of moving away, she slid a hand around the back of his neck, and her fingers wandered into his hair. She felt as if she were sinking into a whirling abyss where escape was impossible. "Unwise," she whispered, but her body went soft against his. She liked the way she felt in his arms. He was solid, sturdy, comforting. What did she want? Another taste of his kiss? A relief for the throbbing inside her? As if reading her mind, he tugged her close as if he had a right.

Tipping her head back, she searched his eyes for only a second. Her lips parted invitingly beneath the gentle pressure of his. Why did it feel so good, so right to be in his arms? Why did she feel as if only he could take her on a once-in-a-lifetime adventure? Desire was a part of life. She'd never ignored it nor had she ever felt so caught up in a need for any man that it pained her. None of this was supposed to happen, but he was exciting—more exciting than she'd expected, and at some point, he'd kindled a blaze that had smoldered as if waiting for this moment.

The lips playing across hers with a skilled caress inflamed her with a swiftness that left her breathless. She heard a moan—her own—and she realized that all the reasons that she'd shoved at herself for days seemed wasted with this one kiss, with the caress of his hand. He made her forget the one thing that she was certain she wanted in her life. He made her question the freedom she needed. He made her world tilt, yet the rock solid hold of his embrace, the sturdiness of his body, the firmness of his kiss steadied her. She saw no logic in what was happening between them. More kisses, more moments like this seemed useless. But as simple as it sounded, there remained one glitch. No matter how much she knew that they were wrong for each other, she wanted him. Burying her face against his neck, she breathlessly struggled to ask, "What do you want?"

The same question had flashed through his mind more than once lately. For a man who'd planned his life carefully, the question was unsettling. "You," he murmured while he slid his hands beneath her blouse.

Where he touched her, she tingled, weakened, she thought in amazement. "This is—"

"Yeah, I know," he said, slowly unbuttoning her blouse.

She felt his smile against her throat. "Josh." His name came out on a whisper in unison with the rustle of silk as her blouse slipped from her shoulders. "You're too brilliant not to understand—"

"So are you," he said, not needing to open his eyes to see the books stacked in a corner of the room. Books that ranged from the philosophies of the

Chinese political movement to the study of Cézanne and Renoir.

"You're ambitious," she reminded him even as her lips grazed his cheekbone.

He stood and drew her up to him. "Definitely an unpleasant trait."

"To me, it is. And—" She stopped as her skirt floated to the floor.

Differences didn't matter to him. He saw only one problem. He wanted a home. He needed roots. She didn't. "Are you afraid?" he asked softly, framing her face with his hands.

Frightened? Yes, she was. He touched her heart. He made her forget everything she'd promised herself years ago.

With a thumb, he caressed her cheek. "Of a touch?"

As he leaned forward and brushed her lips with his mouth, she grabbed a deep breath.

"Of a kiss?" he whispered.

"Josh, I—" Her voice sounded breathless even to her ears.

"Want me," he murmured against her hair as he lifted her into his arms and carried her into the bedroom. With every breath he drew, her scent intoxicated him a little more. For the moment, this moment, he wanted to drown in that fragrance. "I want you."

She clung, aware of his strength, of her weakness for him. Why did anything have to matter but the taste of his lips, of his tongue, of the warm recesses of his mouth? Nothing did, she realized as she listened to the beating drum of her own heart, its rhythm quick while it pumped blood faster. When he drew back so his eyes met hers in the faint light of her bedroom, she no longer could resist what she wanted as much as he did.

As he lowered her to the bed and she tilted her head back to look at him, his gaze followed the creamy flesh exposed at the lace of her bra. Nothing could be softer, he thought, pressing his lips to the shadowed skin. "I ache for you."

She was lost with a longing she'd never felt for any man before. She pushed aside niggling concerns. All that mattered was the moment. When his bare flesh brushed against hers, desire controlled her. She'd never missed it through the years until that moment. Now, she felt she would die for a touch, to touch.

She couldn't speak. The soft whispering sound of his voice enticed and urged her. Lightly her hands roamed over a back as strong as the man. Languidly she caressed the muscular flesh of his hip. As he shifted, she tantalizingly grazed his chest with her fingertips, splaying them to feel as much of the muscles and the smoothness as she could. When she reached his stomach, she felt him quiver, and with the power he offered her, heat pounded through her. It was like a fire, and instead of running from it, she welcomed it.

Their lips came together as if they were starving. Twisting, his mouth possessed hers with a promise while his tongue deepened the kiss as if he were trying to immerse himself in her. As passion flickered and then demanded, differences suddenly didn't matter.

Only his mouth—warm, persuasive, stirring. Only his hands—caressing, stroking, enticing. Only the need—mindless, pleasurable, aching.

This was the intimacy that she'd never thought she wanted again. But then had she ever had it with anyone like this?

The chill of night danced across her bare flesh yet only the heat within her body mattered. She was a creature of need as his mouth found her breast to taunt and please her. Lingeringly his lips roamed over her then moved lower while his hands sought her every curve.

She was wild beneath his touch, controlled by an urgency that matched his. With persisting slowness, with fluttering quickness, as if memorizing every inch of her, he challenged her. On a moan, he shifted, his tongue gliding down her skin, flicking at it until she thought she would strangle with madness. Her body molded to his strong hands, captivated by their gentleness and their pressure, seduced by a featherlight caress or a demanding stroke. When he lowered his head and filled himself with the taste of her, she was caught up in a dark, encompassing, pleasurable torment. She wanted to rest, needed to catch her breath, and all the while, he urged her on with every tender touch of his moist tongue.

As his mouth raced upward, across the smoothness of her belly, over her breasts to the curve of her neck, she was whirled into another world. In desperation, she arched toward him. The need for another person wasn't supposed to carry such pain, such agony, such hunger. She'd known passion's abandonment before. But never like this. It pleasured and weakened her. The world didn't exist outside. This man, she realized, gasping with a breathless excitement, he was her world.

At her shudder against him, he was beyond thinking. She rushed him, until he was throbbing with sensation. Murmuring her name, he gave up all restraint. He closed his mouth over hers again and tugged her to him. He'd wanted her like this from the beginning. He'd tasted beyond his own desire, riding on her pleasure, insisting, wanting her to know his need for her went beyond passion's edge. He'd devoured with a craving that he'd never known. Never would feel for another, he realized. He'd sought every inch of her. He'd wanted to seduce her. He'd wanted to make her ache, make her yearn as much as he did. He was a man of discipline, he'd told himself, and he'd lost all patience. She made him senseless to everything but the sensation wrenching his gut.

On a moan he entered her. Flesh blended with flesh. The sound of her soft sigh exploded in his mind. As she wrapped around him passion coiled even tighter. On a gasp, he caught his breath like a drowning man then gave in to it, letting it pull him under.

Pleasure was their mutual need. They drove each other until they were bathed in a sultry heat. Moving against him, with him, for him, she clung, binding him to her. With an abandonment that rocked her world, he hurled her upward with him. And she floated. Floated with a freedom she'd never known before.

Disoriented, Josh's first coherent thought amusingly was that he would never breathe normally again. He lay in a jumble of sheets and shifted only to ease his weight from her. On an exhausted breath, he drew her tight to him. His eyes shut, he gave in to his senses, responding to the heat of the morning sun on his face, comforted by the weight of her head on his shoulder, the dampness of her body, the caress of her fingers on his chest. How close could he bring her to him before she ran? It was a question that he didn't want to think about. She was the softness and the sweetness and the brightness that had been missing in his world, and he tightened her to him, cherishing every second that he did have with her.

As he stretched his legs, they made contact with her slim, long ones. Eyes still closed, he rolled toward her. "Beautiful lady," he murmured, scooting down and seeking the soft curve of her collarbone.

Allie drew a long breath, her stomach muscles tightening in response to his lips' descent, and the hot and quick sensations of his breath against her flesh as his mouth grazed it. A slow-moving heat swept over her with the gentle touch of his hands skimming her hips and thighs while his lips teased her breast.

As he lowered his head and his tongue trailed the same path as his hand, she couldn't remain still. He lured her down a path filled with more excitement than she'd ever anticipated. Gliding her hands over his flesh, she absorbed its smoothness and its heat, and impatience overwhelmed her. Her one thought, her only thought, was to have him again, to feel him filling her, blending himself with her until a oneness she'd never really shared with another existed again. On a quiet shudder, she gripped at his shoulders, and giving in to the sensations cascading through her, she opened her body to his in welcome invitation.

When he awoke, he couldn't say if he'd slept minutes or hours. All sense of time had slipped away. For a long time, he lay still. A contentment that he hadn't believed existed filled him. He moved his hand across the sheet, searching for her. A sense of loss registered first, then an easier one settled over him with the scent of coffee. He found her in the kitchen, bathed in the soft glow of morning sunlight.

She never heard his approach, but the sound of footsteps weren't needed. The gentle hand, possessive and steady, skimming up her thigh, swayed her back as if she were meant to be a part of him. She'd awakened with conflicting emotions. Dazed, she'd wondered how this closeness had come so quickly. Why it had. She'd always been so certain that she would keep her life free of binding ties. With a man like him nothing was casual. He charged toward permanency with the same intensity that she retreated from it. She felt ecstatic and concerned at the same time. Everything she'd believed before seemed far away. But now wasn't the time to wonder why. Facing him, feeling his arms around her again, she scrambled to dodge the one emotion. She'd accept mutual need as their binding force. She wouldn't spoil the time with him. "Coffee is done," she murmured. The arm curled around her tightened and pulled her even closer.

"That wasn't the taste I needed." As he kissed a corner of her lips, he noted the cloud of worry in her eyes. Too many words rushed his brain to convey his feelings. "Don't be sorry," he appealed, pushing strands of hair away from her face with his thumbs.

Allie leaned into him on a soft laugh. "I'm not," she assured him. "Not at all. I was thinking how many hours it would be before you come home again."

"Too many," he said thickly. At her reminder of the time, he reluctantly released his hold to let her turn away. Even as he stepped away, her scent, her taste, her softness lingered in his memory. Though other women eagerly longed for reassuring words, they were the words that she would shy from. He had no choice, he realized, except to take one moment at a time. But he swore under his breath. He was feeding himself a lot of bull. He wanted to spend hours listening to her, touching her, being with her just like this.

"You have time for breakfast, don't you?" she asked, rummaging through several cabinets as if on a scavenger hunt.

He shoved aside thoughts that he believed in about vows and promises with the same quickness that he gave up his search of sugar for his coffee. She wouldn't want to hear them. And because he wasn't sure he wanted to say them, because a semblance of orderliness was imbedded in him, he forced himself to back off. At the clatter of the skillet she'd set on the stove burner, he frowned. "I have to ask."

She swung a look back at him, a mixing bowl in her hands.

"What are you making? Because if it's spaghetti or tuna or—well, I'll pass."

She cracked a smile. "Never let it be said that I don't understand the order of things."

He stretched out on a chair and watched her stroll to the stove. She was slender, small in the hips and breasts and long-legged. She was exquisite, he thought not for the first time. "What's the order of things?"

"The knight rescued the damsel last night. In return, he received lodging for the night." Slowly her head swiveled over her shoulder to look at him. "And received some pleasures from the daughter of the host. And now he receives food before he goes on his way."

"Such as—"

She laughed. "How about blueberry pancakes?"

He looked upward. "Thank you for that."

When he started toward the door, she set the mixing bowl on the counter. "With bran and sesame seeds."

Josh groaned.

"Where are you off to?"

He paused in the doorway and looked back at her. "A shower."

"Be careful." She winked meaningfully. "You never know who'll walk in on you."

A lazy, pleased grin turned up the corners of his lips. "I'll give you five minutes."

"Who said I was joining you?" she teased.

"You have a subtle wink."

"That wasn't a wink. It was a twitch."

He braced a hand against the doorjamb and grinned at her. "That's an attractive twitch, you have. But you might as well give up your act. You've been wanting to join me in the shower since the first day we met in that cramped room."

"Have I?"

"Admit it," he said turning away, "you've got a thing for the nice, boring, dull types."

If only he was, she mused. He was steady and stable and intelligent. And he was daring and exciting and incredibly sexy. Unbeatable combination, she thought on a sigh.

Chapter Eight

Josh arrived at the college seconds before a drizzle began. Softly, rain tapped at the windows during his first class. Through his second, the sound of thunder rumbled overhead. By the time he was passing out reading lists to the last few students filing out of his room, the storm had broken, and a downpour drummed against the cement.

"It isn't a day fit for a fish," Nate said, strolling in.

On a smile, Josh looked up from stacking papers and shoving them into his briefcase for grading.

"I considered waiting until lunch to talk to you, but that incredibly nosy Tuborn is always sitting nearby."

"Ah, your arch rival."

"The loquacious fool. He's an untapped source of natural gas."

Josh waited for the punch line.

"An overabundance of hot air."

He smiled at Nate. "You shouldn't let him get to you."

"I imagine," he grumbled, "that Tuborn will insist on sitting near me during the faculty dinner."

Frowning, Josh stared in puzzlement at him.

"What's this?" Nate asked in surprised tone. "You forgot that Saturday evening is the faculty dinner?"

Josh swore under his breath. "I've been preoccupied," he admitted.

"I assume you won't be coming alone."

Would he be? Would Allie want to go with him? Josh wondered.

"I'm not certain how much you've been aware of lately," Nate said in a teasing tone. "But I've decided to resign."

Josh whipped around, sending the books on his desk sliding across it.

A gleam of laughter danced in Nate's eyes. "As matchmaker. You've obviously found what you want. A bright red balloon on any faculty car is an unusual sight."

"And what's the reaction?"

"You're young and susceptible to certain maladies."

Josh restacked the books. "Such as?"

"Being smitten." Nate chuckled. "I tell everyone who asks that she's lovely."

"That she is." Josh met his stare. "Nate, she could be the one."

Nate's head jerked back slightly. "You're jesting?" Frowning, he perched on the edge of Josh's desk. "But she's not—"

"Right for the image?" Josh finished.

"I wouldn't say that but—"

"You don't have to tell me. I've had similar arguments with myself," Josh admitted.

"My boy." Nate placed a firm hand over his shoulder. "This could be merely lust."

Josh considered how easy that would make everything. "Could be," he said to ease away Nate's frown.

"I only meant that you might be mistaking one emotion for another."

Josh gave him a reassuring grin, aware that Nate meant well. "I don't think so, but she and I both know that we're not right for each other."

Sympathetically Nate sighed before he started toward the door. As he reached the doorway, he stopped and looked back. His worried frown still in place, he reminded Josh, "Don't forget. There's also a faculty meeting at six-thirty today."

Josh looked away in annoyance. He wouldn't get home before Allie left for the radio station. Outside, a slanting sheet of rain pelted the ground. Gray and gloomy, the weather matched his mood.

When had she ever felt such disappointment at not seeing a particular man? Allie wondered later that night, a night that dragged by.

While a series of songs played, she strolled out of the broadcasting booth toward her office to find a misplaced promotional sheet about dog food. Though she strived for as little regimentation as possible in her life, in her work, she was organized. Meticulously she'd rechecked her script before airtime. She'd had the sponsor's promo with her other sheets. Annoyed at herself, she rummaged through several drawers of her desk before she raced to the file cabinet.

Earlier, she'd scanned previous nights' scripts with her private notations on them. Because boredom killed any broadcast, she reread old scripts to prevent repetitive playing of any song two nights in a row. She'd checked her playing log before airtime. The promo had to be in that file.

With only two minutes left, she quickly yanked out the file folder and began thumbing through the papers. If the dog food commercial wasn't in the file then— On a sigh of relief, she closed her fingers over the missing promo. But in less than a heartbeat, a realization settled over her. The papers in the file folder were out of order.

Frowning, Allie glanced at the clock. With one minute and five seconds left, she had to get back to the broadcasting booth. She snatched up the promo script, shoved the file folder in the drawer, slammed it and raced down the hall. She flicked on the microphone with three seconds to spare, but she spent hours wondering who had been nosing in her files and why.

At three-thirty, Kirby arrived at the station to take over the microphone. Standing beside him, talking excitedly, Neil waved at her. They'd made the demo the day before, and Neil had shipped it by overnight mail to Los Angeles.

While Madonna was wailing out a song, Neil poked his head in the broadcasting room. "The offer came through. Sort of," he added.

He strolled to her, his eyes and complexion bright with excitement.

"From Los Angeles," he said when she didn't respond. "All we have to do is wait for the big shots to make a final decision."

She tugged at her bottom lip. Why wasn't she as pleased or as excited as he was?

"They heard us and thought we were great," he said, too caught up in his own delight to notice her hesitation. "I was told that they'll let us know for sure in a few days."

"Are they offering a contract? How long will the job be for?"

"How long?" he stared at her as if she were crazy.

"Yes, how long?"

"Nothing is steady in this business."

She knew that. And she'd never wondered before how long she would be anywhere. It had never mattered.

"Who cares? We accept this. If we don't like it, we'll go somewhere else. That's the way it always is. But this is a great stepping stone, Allie." At her silence his enthusiasm wound down. "What's the matter with you? No strings. No commitments. You always said that."

She finished stacking her papers. "I know what I said. But I'm not so glib about starving. We could be there a month. If ratings fall, we're out. I'm not apathetic about where my next paycheck will come from."

"Since when did you become so hung up on security?"

She heard anger in his voice and reached out to touch his arm. He stepped back, preventing the contact. "Neil, I'm not concerned about—"

"Sure sounds like it to me. In fact, you've been acting funny lately."

"I haven't been acting funny. I thought it was a great opportunity but—" Unconsciously she swiveled her chair away and reached down for her purse under the console. "But I'm not sure."

"What is it with you?" he yelled.

"Neil, I'm not sure," Allie said with as much calm as she could muster. "You told me that they had a single slot open, too. Even if I don't go, you would still have a job. If they liked your sound on our demo, then they like you. They'd offer the other job to you."

"That one isn't prime time. It's not a morning show, Allie."

A hint of accusation edged his voice. She felt a slow moving chill sweep over her. How had this happened? she wondered. She'd fled her family's demands only to walk right back into a similar situation. When had his expectations stretched over to make demands on her? She turned away. "I'll let you know," she said firmly over her shoulder, not comfortable with his insistence.

"Soon," he insisted.

Allie glanced back at his angry face.

"You'll never get a golden opportunity like this again," he shot back.

In what seemed a deliberate act, he waited until she flicked the switch and was on the air before he let the door slam loudly behind him. Allie kept her anger restrained, but she was still fuming when Kirby took over the mike.

Walking through the hallway to the women's restroom, she wondered if she would want to team with someone like Neil. Whether he was angry or not, he'd lacked professionalism, or he wouldn't have done that to her.

Even though she dreaded the necessary confrontation, she left the restroom and strolled toward the offices to find him.

Standing in the parking lot outside KFKQ's building, Josh shoved back the cuff of his jacket and peered at his watch. When Allie hadn't come home by six that morning, he'd driven to the radio station. Impatiently he glanced at her car still parked near the building's door.

Fifteen minutes later, he decided to take his chances that he would get in without a security bell screeching a warning of an intruder.

Behind the glass walls of the broadcasting booth, the morning deejay swiveled his chair from one desk to another, all the while maintaining his rapid monologue.

Bill Vannen, Jr. was at a desk in one of the facing rooms. He was staring catatonically at the deejay while an older man, a more rotund version of Junior, talked. Josh watched the man's flapping mouth. He didn't need to hear the conversation to guess that the senior Vannen was giving his son a tongue-lashing.

With a turn down the next hall, he saw Allie standing at the end of it and talking to Neil. Josh forced himself to plant his feet and wait for her.

Allie found Neil instantly apologetic.

A sheepish smile remained plastered on his face. "I'm sorry about what happened. I acted like a real ass," he said. "But I was excited."

In her family's eyes, Allie had done stupid things when excited, and no one had understood that she'd been swept away by her own emotion. "I know you are," she said understandingly. "And I'm sorry that I'm dragging my feet about this, but I follow intuition, and something about the move to Los Angeles, about this job, doesn't hit me right."

"Nerves." Grinning, Neil grabbed her hand and squeezed it encouragingly. "You're just nervous, baby. California is a big audience. But don't be a fool, Allie." He paused and looked past her, making her aware Josh was waiting for her. "Don't let him make you hesitate."

As he put his arm around her shoulder and bent his head close to hers, she struggled to return a token smile.

"You'll write your own ticket after this. You'll be a household name in Los Angeles. You'll be a success. Everyone wants that."

Allie reared back. "Do they?"

"Sure. Everyone."

Words that were meant to convince her scared the daylights out of her. "Him, too?" she asked, stepping away from Neil to gesture with her head in Chad's direction. "Is that why he's burning the candle at both ends?"

"Huh?" Neil turned a puzzled look on her.

"Chad," she said emphatically. "He's working overtime. I've seen him here close to midnight and at four in the morning," she added as an explanation.

"He's not working overtime."

"He—" She paused. "He was here at four the other morning."

"He shouldn't have been." What sounded like a mirthless laugh slipped out. "I wonder if he's got big ideas or the hots for you?"

Allie swung a frown at him.

He raised his brows in a speculative expression. "It's possible, Allie. You should report him though. Security is tight at this place. Vannen wouldn't be happy to hear that Chad was here when he wasn't supposed to be."

The click of footsteps made her look up. As Chad strolled away, she shook her head. "No, I don't want to get him in trouble."

Minutes seemed like hours before she turned away to meet him, Josh thought. When Neil had slipped an arm around Allie's shoulder, Josh had battled a pang of jealousy with some reassuring nonsense that the hug was nothing more than brotherly affection, but he'd felt edgy for her. He'd seen the gawky, surly-looking kid that she'd called Chad standing in a corner watching her. Just watching her.

More than jealousy nudged him then. The need to protect her was strong again. From what? The lecherous Vannen Jr., the kid whose eyes had never left her, or the man she'd been talking to?

Neil was a greater danger to Josh. Neil could take her from him. "That's quite a crew you work with," Josh said later when they strolled up the stairs to his apartment. "Junior has tentacles instead of hands and—"

"Uh, huh," she answered distractedly while sorting through her previous day's mail.

"That jerky deejay—"

Allie swung a smile up at him. "Are we talking about Neil now?"

The tension hadn't eased away. He felt it in his neck and shoulders. Muscles knotted and burned. "He's too familiar."

"What's the definition of familiar?"

"Mine or *Webster's*?"

"They aren't the same?"

"I don't have the exact meaning from the dictionary but—"

She tsked at him.

Josh ignored her intent to gibe. "But I see a man who's too damn possessive," he said with some annoyance. "He touches you all the time."

"So does Junior."

"Not in the same way. Neil would take over if you let him," he warned.

"But I won't let him."

"And that other guy," Josh went on, troubled that so many men cluttered her life.

Facing him, Allie dropped the mail into her purse and leaned back against the wall. "Who are we talking about now?"

"The kid who's always hanging around corners."

"Chad."

He rocked a hand before unlocking the door. "Something isn't right there, either."

"If anyone heard you, they'd say you're paranoid."

"I don't give a damn what they'd think or say. My concern is for you."

Her eyes slanted skeptically at him.

"Okay, I'll admit it. I'm jealous," he said, pushing the door open harder than necessary. "And concerned. They go hand-in-hand sometimes. I don't like those—"

She placed a finger to his lips to silence him, not wanting to have to defend anyone at the moment. "Some of them aren't my favorite people, either. But you work with people that you don't care for, don't you?"

"Yes," he admitted, his thoughts shifting to the boring Tuborn.

She strolled further into the room. He was meticulous. In the short time since Josh had arrived, he'd worked hard to turn the apartment into a home. Shelves of orderly lined books covered one of the black walls of his living room. A tract of overhead lights radiated brightness along the window wall. Gone was the previous owner's moss-green sofa. Replacing it were two beige, soft-cushioned ones. On the gleaming wood floor was a room-size throw rug with an Indian design in shades of beige, white and black. Her back to him, she stared at the framed map on the wall. "What is this map?"

Though he wanted to shake some sense into her, instead, he gently curled a hand over her shoulder. "It's the Oregon Trail."

Allie focused at the lines on the yellowed paper. "Is this a copy?"

"An original."

She released a semblance of a soft whistle. "Expensive item."

Splaying a palm over her belly, he inched closer. "Well, worth what I spent."

She wasn't surprised that he'd value something historically significant. As he pulled her back to him, she laid her head on his shoulder. "Those must have been difficult times."

He sighed in resignation. She was too much her own person for him to force anything on her. Featherlight he traced a slow path with his tongue over the shell of her ear. "They battled storms and Indians and drought."

She brushed a hand at her ear. "To find something new and different," she said with her usual optimism.

"They gave up everything that they'd known," he countered, turning her in his arms to face him.

"Because they thought that they'd find something better." Slowly he smiled at her in that confident way that tended to unbalance her.

Josh shook his head. "Wrong answer."

She couldn't help but laugh. "I failed the test?"

"You were misinformed."

She smiled up at him. "Okay, what's the right answer?"

"They left to find a place they could call their home."

Home. He placed so much importance on it. Didn't he realize that a person could have a home and still not have a sense of belonging?

At her silence, he knew he'd struck the raw spot between them. What could he say to make her see things differently?

Allie inclined her head and then casually draped one arm over his shoulder while she mirrored his scowl. "Why the frown?"

Josh dodged confrontation. To have her with him now was all that mattered. "I have to go to a faculty dinner on Saturday evening." He rested his hands on the sharp points of her hips. "Go with me," he urged, lazily stroking her back.

"That's unfair. You're taking advantage—"

"Any time I can."

Allie narrowed her eyes at him. "Is this something you learned during all those years of schooling?"

"I'm a history teacher. I know all about strategic maneuvers."

As his fingers strayed downward to the curve of her hip, she laughed. "I'll bet you do. But I don't think I should go with you. These are the people who really count, aren't they?"

His whisper fanned her cheek. "You're the one that counts."

He turned her to mush with a few words. She couldn't pretend that she didn't want to be with him whenever she could. "I'll go," she said on a long breath that was meant to sound suffering.

"I'll have to remember your weakness."

Her hand slid across his chest. "Your strategy won out."

"This?" he asked, his tongue grazing the flesh of her neck.

On a sigh, she closed her eyes. "You said that the evening included dinner, didn't you?"

"Is that an incentive?"

Scooting closer, she curled an arm around his neck and pressed her body against him. "Free food is never a deterrent."

"How about dancing?"

Rearing back, she slanted a look at him. "There'll be dancing?"

"The minuet," he said deadpan.

"Oh, that's a relief." She held back a grin. "I don't know how to fox-trot."

His head went back with laughter. "Neither do I."

"I suppose it's a simple step or two," she said, moving her hips and brushing against him.

He drew a sharp breath. "We could practice."

"To music?"

"Uh, huh," he said, distracted by her fingers on his chest, playing with a shirt button.

"In the bedroom?"

"Better yet." He slipped his hands beneath her blouse and felt the velvety soft skin at her waist. "We could forget going and stay here." His voice trailed off as his own words rushed back at him.

At the dumbfounded look that settled in his face, she couldn't help but smile. "Surprised yourself, didn't you?" she guessed.

Stunned, he wondered if he'd gaped. There had been a time before he'd met her when he'd never have considered missing a social evening with colleagues. "It's your fault," he chided lightly. "You make me senseless."

"Not the best thing for a man of knowledge."

He tightened his arms on her back and held her so close that they had to breathe as one. "But inevitable for a man who's smitten."

"Smitten?" She laughed.

His smile reached his eyes. "That's the gossip around Wainwright."

"It is?" she asked on a tease, but she didn't want words. She wanted him. She needed the strength that she'd become familiar with, the gentleness that lulled her, the hunger that she'd begun to crave.

As she leaned into him, her fingers floating downward, he needed no more encouragement. When he crushed her to him and captured her lips and the taste of her filled his mouth, a madness spiraled through him. He would never get enough of her. Never. He buried his face in her hair and drew her into the bedroom with him. Words clinging to his tongue were never said. Her mouth was on his again. Swift and demanding, desire mingled into his love for her. An urgency swept him beneath a torrent of passion. Caresses changed and became demands. And the headiness of pleasure took over. It wasn't the first time, and Josh vowed it wouldn't be the last for them.

Sunshine filled the room before Josh eased himself from her side. Her breathing slow and even, she shifted on the bed to where he'd been. She looked young and vulnerable and enticing. For an instant, he considered sliding back under the sheet, but he was a creature of habit. Stifling several yawns, he slid on clothes and strolled toward the door for his morning run while he tried to remember if he'd done his lecture for his first class at ten.

At the click of the door, Allie rolled over to hug his pillow. With every breath she drew, she absorbed his scent. She'd been an innocent before. Virginity had been lost years ago, but she'd never emotionally given so much to any man. Desire had never done more than warm her body. He made it touch her heart, caress every fiber of her.

She burrowed herself deeper under the covers and tried to go back to sleep. Ten minutes later with the quiet slam of the apartment door, she was still tired and still awake. If she was tired, he had to be, yet he'd managed to haul himself from the bed to jog.

As he entered the bedroom, she slitted her eyes at him. Wearing a sweatshirt, jogging shorts, and sneakers, he was bathed in sweat. Though she'd never been susceptible to bodybuilders, their skin sheening and bulging, she felt the quick prick of desire as she stared at him. If only desire were all that she felt. If she only yearned or craved for him, the answer would be simple. Lust was fleeting. Something that could be savored and set aside. But he'd become important to her. Necessary. "Kind of cold outside for those shorts, isn't it?"

Turning at the foot of the bed to face her, he brushed a hand at his damp face. "Is it?"

The muscles in his thighs were hard and long, pumped up from the exercise. Disciplined always, she mused. He'd never hid his need for schedules and certainties. And she'd never wanted either.

"Hey?" He peeled off his sweatshirt and then braced his arms on each side of her. "Lazy lady," he teased, bending forward to lightly kiss her mouth.

"I warned you that I was."

He smiled down at her. "You look fantastic like this."

She narrowed an eye at him while running her hands over his back. She found the musky scent clinging to him as arousing as his clean, showered one. "Being lazy? Looking sleepy? Or what?"

He lowered his head and ran light, taunting kisses across her shoulder to the edge of the sheet. Soft. Her skin was soft as velvet everywhere. He pressed one last kiss at the hollow between her breasts. Stepping back, he studied her impish grin and then winked. "Naked."

She laughed as he turned away. Beneath her the sheet felt cool where he hadn't been. She nuzzled into a warmer spot. Even when he wasn't near, she wanted a part of him. When had that happened? Why had she allowed it? She'd always been so sure of not what she wanted, but of what she hadn't wanted. Suddenly she wasn't sure of anything except that she might be in love with him.

Josh closed his eyes and faced the shower nozzle to let the spray rush over his head. When had he ever wanted to relax and just enjoy the day, do nothing?

By the time he entered the kitchen in her apartment, he hadn't any answers to what she stirred in him. He'd pursued, aware that she'd been right when she'd insisted they were too different. But when he was with her, those differences didn't exist.

Allie drained the bacon strips before looking back at him. One by one, he was opening and closing cupboard doors. "What are you looking for?"

"The sugar bowl."

"Oh. There are a few packets of sugar in that cabinet," she said with a jabbing motion of her arm.

"Packets? Like restaurant packets?"

"I don't use sugar in my coffee or iced tea. So whenever I go to a restaurant, I feel that I'm entitled to two packets every visit."

He turned away, his shoulders moving in silent mirth.

"You're laughing at me, aren't you?"

"With you," he assured her, amusement still lingering in his voice. But he only spoke the words; he wasn't laughing.

As he reached into the cabinet for the sugar, the mail on the counter below it caught his eye. One letter paralyzed him. "What is this?" Josh read the paper with its cutout letters pasted to it. The message was simple and crude. A message that was meant to frighten, to make her leave Barrington. "Bastard," he said quietly.

"I got it yesterday," she said. Shocked when she'd received the letter, she honestly hadn't known what to do with it. And she'd been fighting the initial shivers of fear ever since. "Breakfast will be ready in—"

"Stop it!" He moved beside her and bent slightly so their eyes were level. "I'm not leaving until we figure out what to do about this," he said, dropping the letter on the counter as if his fingers had been burned.

"But your classes—"

"They can be canceled today. Why didn't you tell me about this?"

Her reasoning had been simple. If she didn't allow herself to think spooky thoughts then she wouldn't fall apart. Someone who barreled toward challenges would never understand that, she realized, so she didn't try to explain to him.

"Call the police," he said, offering her the telephone receiver.

"Josh—" She started to protest with a shake of her head.

"Call them," he said firmly. "Or I will."

"Nothing we can do about this," the uniformed officer said, setting the sheet of paper back on the kitchen counter.

"Why can't you?" Josh asked with a calmness that he didn't feel.

"It's not really a threat on her life. It could be a prank."

Allie sent him an I-told-you-so look.

"And it might not be," Josh insisted, ignoring her.

"That's true, it might not be. But until something happens that's more—"

"Dangerous," Josh finished for the policeman.

"Hey, I realize that these kind of things can seem frightening but they usually aren't anything serious."

"She's had phone calls, too."

The officer shifted toward Allie. "Have you?"

She nodded.

"Could you recognize the voice?"

"No. It was as distinguishable as the handwriting in this letter."

The officer laughed at her obvious attempt to lighten the moment. Josh glared at him.

"I'll file the report," he said quickly. "And if you have anything else—"

"Why can't you check for fingerprints?" Josh asked.

"It probably wouldn't do any good. Too many people have touched the paper. And the character who takes the time to cut out these letters would wear gloves. So if anything else happens," he said, heading for the door, "call."

Josh waited only until they were alone. "How can you take this so lightly?"

How could she explain that she'd programmed herself to ignore the unpleasant side of life. By not taking life too seriously, she'd weathered years of standing and listening to praises about her sisters, months of Kyle nagging her to act differently and hours of well-meaning phone calls from family members about her life-style. "Someone has a warped sense of humor, Josh. I can't let that affect me. Things like this happen to deejays."

A frown etched a deep crease between his brows. "Often?"

"Occasionally. Deejays are likely targets. I told you before that I thought this person was nothing more than a prankster," she assured him, placing a hand on his chest. "Relax. Okay?"

"No." He shook his head. "Not knowing who's doing this is your biggest problem. Look, I checked about the flowers."

"You checked?"

"I checked."

Of course, he would, she realized.

"There was no way to find out who sent them. It was a cash transaction from a florist in another town." He drew a hard breath. "Call the phone company and change your number, Allie."

"Oh, Josh—" she started.

"Call the phone company and tell them to come out," he said firmly as she continued to stare at him. "Dammit, do something," he appealed angrily, feeling a helplessness that trembled him.

She relied on his good sense this time. To make her own decision meant pondering over a problem that she didn't want to consider overlong.

While she made the call, he strolled out to the terrace with a cup of coffee. He needed to reason with her, make her sense the danger that was near. How could she be so carefree at a moment like this? He didn't understand her, he realized not for the first time.

"All done," Allie said. "But the phone company told me that they wouldn't be out here for days."

He muttered a low curse then opened his arms to her.

For a long moment, she accepted the solace of his embrace. Anxiety coiled a tight knot within her. As the strong arms around her remained firmly in place, she felt the tenseness in his body. He was angry at her, but he always accepted and welcomed her into his arms without hesitation.

"Are you really okay?" he murmured against her hair.

Though more nervous than she wanted to admit even to herself, she forced a weak smile forward. "I'm fine." At the concern clouding his eyes, she insisted, "Really."

"Come on, then," he said, turning away and drawing her with him toward the door.

Trailing him, Allie accepted the moment as a lighthearted one. "Where?"

"I want you to stay at my place."

As they reached the door of her apartment, she balked slightly. "Josh, don't be silly."

"Don't be dumb." He tugged her with him.

"You're overreacting."

"Fine. Call it what you want. But I want you stay at my place."

Allie shook her head. "I'm paying rent for that—" She let her words trail off as he drew her with him down the hall to his apartment. "Josh, are you listening?"

He didn't answer until they stood inside his apartment and the door was closed behind them. "I'm listening. I'm listening to my heart pound every time I think about you in some kind of danger. Don't be stubborn." He grabbed her arms. "And listen to me. Someone—whoever it is—knows where you live. Is that common knowledge over the air?"

Allie avoided his eyes.

"So it's someone you know." He loosened his grip and ran his thumbs soothingly over her arms, hoping he hadn't bruised them.

If her legs weren't shaking, she would move. But until that moment, she hadn't considered that she personally knew the person. Only someone who knew her could have phoned her, could have known where to send those flowers, that wreath, the letter.

Chapter Nine

He watched her circle his living room as if suddenly caged. Nervous tension held her back straight, almost rigid. "I finally stirred a scare in you, didn't I?"

"Yes," she admitted. Someone she knew had done everything. She'd slipped on blinders deliberately or she'd have accepted the fact sooner, but he hadn't. All this time, he'd considered that possibility. No wonder he was edgy about so many people.

"You can take anything you want lightly, Allie. I don't care. But some things require tough, serious talk, and this is one of them. Who do you think is doing it?"

She turned a puzzled look at him.

"Have you had any more phone calls?"

"Not recently." Panic fluttered her stomach. How stupid she'd been to think that it was someone who didn't like her program, someone who would eventually call and air his complaints to management. The solution had sounded so simple then.

"Consider who might be a likely culprit," he insisted. A dozen emotions flitted across her face. He realized that she wasn't dodging her problem; she was gathering strength to face it. He'd seen the realistic side of her. She dressed warmly, ate healthy, exercised. Beneath the airiness that she presented to everyone was a woman with her feet planted firmly. "Allie." He spoke softly.

She realized that she wasn't ready. As if someone had dumped water on her to shock her, she trembled slightly. When he opened his arms to her, she leaned forward against him, feeling suddenly tired. "You won't leave me alone about this, will you?"

"'Fraid not."

The incredulity she felt edged forward. "I just can't believe someone I know would be doing this."

"Someone is," he said simply. Framing her face, he stroked her pale cheek. "What about Junior?"

She shook her head.

"Why not?"

Allie wrinkled her nose. "Harmless lech."

"Okay, let's go to a more likely suspect. You took someone's job," he reminded her. "What better reason to be angry."

She turned a look up at him. "Sam Bailey left for another job."

"Where?"

"He told me he was going to South Dakota."

"That could be checked. He might still be in town."

"There's no point in checking." While his emotion was high, the hand he placed on her cheek was gentle, a caress. Allie brushed her lips across his knuckles. "No. He left for Albuquerque this morning."

"I thought he had a job in South Dakota?"

"He lied." She frowned slightly. "I understand that he didn't want me to know that he didn't have another position. So he lied."

"But he does now?"

"Yes." Even if they'd had this discussion days ago, she would never have believed that Sam was responsible.

"What about the kid who acts strange around you?"

She'd thought of Chad immediately, but he'd done nothing except pester her, make her nervous.

"Neil," Josh said for no reason except that he didn't like him.

Allie scowled. "Enough," she said with a tinge of anger, shaking her head. "I don't want to do this any more."

"Look, you can't—"

With a quick step around him, she turned her back on him and pointed at the instrument case propped in a corner of the room. "Do you play that?"

He nodded but he was silent for a second. She was too soft, too easily hurt. Is that why she kept relationships casual? Because she cared too much about others?

"What else do you play?"

"Piano."

She waited because the inflection in his voice made his answer sound unfinished.

"A sloppy violin," he admitted.

She smiled. "And what's in the case?"

"A saxophone." He'd forced her to talk about the unpleasantness in her life, and ironically he wanted to dodge his own. As she waited expectantly for him to answer her question, he braced a hand against the bedroom doorframe and called himself coward. "I used to sneak the saxophone outside while my father was sleeping."

"Did he know that?"

"I didn't think so, and my mother was at work, so I thought no one knew."

"But they had?"

"Yes, they'd known. After my father died, she gave me his saxophone. She said that he wanted me to have it. She told me that he'd laughed and said that maybe one day I'd play Blue Moon better." Pausing, he met her gaze again. "It was the only song that I did play well. It was his favorite." He drew a deep breath, realizing he'd never told anyone this much, never had wanted to. "She told me then that he'd known I was taking the saxophone."

"And he never said a word to you?" Allie asked.

"No." He shoved a hand in his pants pocket while he steeled emotions that he'd thought he'd left in his past. "He never stopped me from taking it."

A pained expression settled on his face. Before Allie could offer any token of understanding, he turned away toward the bedroom. "I'll be right back. I have to call the college."

She noticed an unnatural coldness in his voice when he'd discussed his father. Despite the happiness she'd known with Josh, he was a man of the same mold as her family. In time, he would expect more from her. He'd expected something from his father and had never forgiven him for the disappointment. Eventually, wouldn't she disappoint him, too?

Life suddenly was far too complicated, she thought, opening the door. Though she'd agreed to stay at his apartment temporarily, she couldn't spend the day in her bathrobe. She needed clothes.

Allie took one step into the hallway and paused.

His back to her, a man stood before her apartment door, his meaty fist rapping at it.

"Junior?"

He swung around and faced her with a perplexed expression, but self-disgust edged his voice as he mumbled more to himself than her, "I can't even get the apartment number right. I thought this one was yours," he said, gesturing back with his thumb at her apartment door.

"It is," she said quickly. She glanced back, grateful Josh wasn't nearby. One sight of him and Junior would have a field day spreading gossip.

"Oh?" He looked even more puzzled.

So was she. Taking control, Allie walked toward him. "What are you doing here? Were you looking for me?"

Hesitantly he stepped closer. He seemed different. Uncertain. Quieter. "Things aren't going too well at the station," he said, staring at his feet as he approached her. Several feet away, he stopped and hesitated again before meeting her stare. "My father is going to replace me as program director."

It wasn't news to Allie. She'd heard rumors that Vannen Sr., a shrewd businessman, would make that decision soon. Still, she felt compelled to offer some sympathy. "I'm sorry."

"Don't be," he said with a shake of head. "It'll be a relief to get away." Something that resembled hurt more than anger slipped into his voice. "He expected too much from me."

Discomforting moments never failed to pop into her life no matter how hard she struggled to remain detached. Moving around so much had helped her avoid too much involvement with anyone, but lately she seemed unable to escape it.

"He always does," Junior said, pulling her thoughts back to him.

Allie shoved a hand into the pocket of her robe. "I'm sure that he expected no more from you than he thought you were capable of. My family is like that. They push—nudge," she corrected. "I never live up to their expectations, either. But they mean well. Your father is like them. Lots of people are."

"He says that I'm lazy."

Allie didn't like the role he'd placed her in. They didn't know each other well enough for him to confide something that obviously was hurting him. "I don't understand. Why did you come here?" she asked.

"You're like him."

"Like him?" Allie asked in amazement.

"Sure of yourself. I thought you'd understand him, because I sure as hell don't."

"I can't help," Allie assured him. Junior was wrong. She wasn't like his father. She wasn't like anyone in her family. And she definitely had never understood what drove her family, made them crave success so much that nothing else mattered—not happiness, other people's feelings, or love.

Silently Josh stood inside the doorway. That the huge man seemed no threat held him still. But he found himself tensing for no real reason except someone was stirring her frown.

Josh waited until Allie rejoined him, then closed the door behind her. "What did he want?"

"To talk."

"I don't like him." He noted the frown hadn't left her face.

"He's troubled."

"How troubled? Your secret admirer is obviously troubled."

"Junior's not—"

He held up a halting hand. "Who's to guarantee that they aren't one in the same."

"He's not doing such things, Josh." She waved a hand in the air as if to dismiss their discussion. "Forget Junior was here."

"Easier said than done," he muttered under his breath.

Allie's heart went out to Junior. He was still trying to win approval. She'd given up trying to please others. She only needed to please herself, she reflected. But if that was true, then why was it becoming so hard to think exclusively only about herself?

"Allie?"

At Josh's voice, she looked up.

"Stay here." He wondered if he dared make his request.

His eyes were serious and brooding, and they melted her heart. He brushed his thumbs at the edges of her lips as if by touch he could stir a smile. She had never been more aware of anyone else's feelings than she was at that moment.

"Do this for me," he said softly, wondering how it was possible to care so much for someone that the emotion could weaken and strengthen him at the same time.

A request, she thought. Not a demand. He'd made a simple request. Coiling her arms around his neck, she smiled weakly because she sensed he needed to see it. "Is it that important to you?"

"You are," he murmured fiercely against her lips. "You are."

Though Josh skipped his morning class, he couldn't escape a department meeting later that day. He'd barely joined the others when Dean Forsythe approached him.

"I'd like to talk to you in private, Josh. I won't keep you on edge," he said the moment they were alone. "A decision was made about the new department chairman."

Josh heard the dreaded "but."

"Canfield was chosen." As he gestured with an arm toward a leather easy chair, Josh moved forward and then took a seat. "You were favorably considered."

Again the silent "but," Josh mused.

"You had the right background."

His head raised slowly. "The right background?"

The older man settled on a leather settee across from him. "Yes, quite. You've traveled so extensively and seen many of the historical places that you lecture about. You provide added depth to your lectures. Everyone thinks very highly of you. But—"

Josh smiled slightly as the word finally was spoken.

"You're considered a bit young for the position. Canfield has been with us for a long time. Nearly twenty-three years. He will retire shortly. He's acquainted with the necessary demands of the position because he helped his predecessor for several years. He is the best person for the position at this time."

"He's a good man," Josh said honestly.

"Yes, I knew that you'd feel that way." He placed his hand on the arm of the sofa and raised himself to a stand.

As Josh took his cue and walked with him toward the door, the man's hand gripped his shoulder. "Your time will come. Wainwright prides itself on acknowledging the efforts of superb educators. How fortunate you were to be given such a diverse life-style as a child."

Josh stilled and stared at him. "Sir?"

"My own background was that of an Air Force brat," he said, smiling. "We gained so much more than if we'd stayed in one place all of our lives. As a child, I was introduced to more life-styles and cultures before I was sixteen than some people experience in their whole lives. As a man who loves history, you must be grateful for that."

Josh simply nodded.

"You traveled all over the United States, didn't you?"

"Yes," Josh answered as they walked back toward the others.

"And even a little of Europe."

Josh's thirteenth year flashed back at him. He'd hated it. They'd lived in sleazy hotels in Paris and Munich and Barcelona for a whole summer. His father had played in local clubs. His mother had housecleaned. Her only enjoyment had been on Sundays when she'd played the organ at the church. His only enjoyment, wandering alone without friends, had been sight-seeing. He'd realized then that he loved learning about what had happened in the past. During that trip to Europe, history had become an integral part of his life.

"How many languages did you learn?"

"Five," Josh answered mechanically.

"Several of your students mentioned that you offered a special lecture on your own time that would be given in French. Wonderful idea," he said enthusiastically. "I've also heard from foreign students how much easier your classes are because of your ability to communicate fluently with them in their native tongue."

Josh focused on him more intently.

"One young woman from Germany told me that you're quite willing to spend extra time explaining lessons to her in German. We're quite happy to have someone like you at Wainwright."

Through the department meeting, Josh battled to keep his mind on business. A patience he'd nurtured through the years nearly disappeared. The same old discussions took place. The same points were made. The same people grumbled at every one of them. That wasn't stability. It was vegetating.

Still, he wanted his part in their lives. He wanted to help make changes at the college. At the thought, he smiled to himself. What would Allie think about that? He wasn't the one who thrived on change, she was. But it wasn't the same kind of change.

While she wanted to bounce around from town to town, he'd worked too hard to get where he was to live out of suitcases again.

With a ten-minute wait before his last class, he returned to his office and made a long-distance call to his mother.

She'd called twice in the past week to ask if he'd learned anything about the chairmanship. She responded to his news predictably, her voice filling with concern for him. "Are you terribly disappointed?"

"No," he admitted honestly. "I'm not. I thought it was what I wanted most."

"It isn't?" she asked.

"No."

She sighed with heavy exasperation. "Must I pry this from you? Who is she?"

He set his head back on the chair. "How did you know?"

"I know. I've been there, dear. Nothing mattered but your father."

"Nothing?"

"Never," she said easily.

He was quiet for a long moment.

"Josh, is something wrong?"

"You never felt as if you'd given up too much?"

"Given up too—" She started and stopped.

"What about a home? Didn't you want one?"

"Oh, I'd have liked one." Confusion slipped into her voice, but she went on, "I'd have liked neighbors and friends. And I know that you would have liked that. I felt sadder for you than myself."

"And what about you? You had a promising career. What about the symphony?"

"The symphony?" she repeated. The puzzlement in her voice gave way to an airy tone. "I never wanted to play with the symphony. It was so disciplined. And life with your father—well—it was an adventure, wasn't it? We saw so much. I don't think I'll ever forget the gondolas in Italy or the train ride through Kansas." She laughed softly. "Do you remember the train breaking down?"

"The train—" He paused and drew a hard breath. As if a movie suddenly were on a screen before him, memories flashed back at him.

"We were stuck in the middle of nowhere for hours and that lovely man who had the fiddle played songs with your father to entertain all of us. We had such good times, didn't we?" she said wistfully.

Yes, they had, he realized. They'd endured hard times but few moments without laughter. A sad cloud drifted over him. Why had he forgotten?

"Josh?"

"You never expected more, did you?"

"Expected?" Worry slipped into her voice. "We had so much of everything. Why would I expect more?"

"I guess—I don't know," he admitted, baffled by his own thoughts. "At Dad's funeral, Grandma—"

"Oh, Josh. She never liked your father. You didn't pay attention to what your grandmother said, did you?"

"I thought—"

"You didn't," she said almost in disbelief.

In retrospect, he wished that he hadn't, but at some point, he'd clung to his grandmother's angry words. Why had he?

"Josh, I never gave up anything that I really wanted. You do understand that?"

"Yeah," he said quietly, forcing the word forward. "And now?" he asked. "Do you have what you want, Mom?"

"Now?" Her laugh came out softly, easily. "Oh, life is rather exciting. We bought new wallpaper today for the dining room."

We. That simple two-letter word said so much. "We?" Josh asked.

"You'll like Frank."

He responded to her warmth. "I'm looking forward to meeting him," he said honestly. Leaning back in the chair, he finished the conversation with her, but more than her happiness touched him. Memories flashed back. Years of what they'd done without were dulled by what they'd shared together.

Why had he forgotten? He shook his head slowly, not believing it had taken so many years for him to understand. At sixteen, he'd clung to anger. It had been easier than handling the grief and allowing himself to feel the hurt of losing his father.

If he'd faced his feelings he would have realized that his mother had always had everything she'd wanted. She'd needed the adventure his father had brought into her life just as he needed Allie. Checks and balances existed everywhere. That's what he'd seen in his parents' marriage but had forgotten. And whether Allie realized it or not, she needed him when her world turned shaky. They needed to balance each other.

Josh called himself every name for fool. He'd been so obsessed with having what he thought he'd missed that he'd forgotten the most important thing that he'd had—love.

It was nearly six that evening when he climbed the stairs toward his apartment. Remembering Allie's weakness, he'd stopped at Mrs. Schultz's bakery for a dozen of her double chocolate doughnuts. Softly whistling, he dangled the white paper bag from his hand.

Only steps from the landing, the whistle died on his lips as he saw the door to her apartment flung open. Josh rushed forward. Stifling the earthy words on the tip of his tongue, he ran a finger along the doorjamb.

The edge of wood around the lock was jagged and splintered. Nothing prepared him for the singular emotion that charged through him. When younger, he'd sent his own adrenaline pumping with daredevil pastimes. Looking back, he realized that his father had taught him to take chances to get what he wanted, and his mother had taught him lessons in patience. But during all those hair-raising moments in Josh's life, he couldn't ever remember fear. He felt it now—for Allie.

"What's in the bag?" Allie asked as she strolled toward him from the kitchen.

Trying not to overreact, he allowed the softness of her voice to float over him like a soothing wave. "Did anyone get in?"

"No. After you left, I came back here, and this is what I found. Someone used a screwdriver on it, but the lock wasn't jimmied." She stopped beside him in the doorway and pointed at the slivers of wood on the floor. "Mrs. V. saw that and insisted I call the police."

She didn't deserve such harassment. He'd seen her with people. He'd heard her on the radio. She offended no one. So why was someone determined to strike fear in her? "What were you doing here?" he asked suddenly, his anger spilling over and mingling with a fierce need to protect her.

Slipping one arm around his waist to urge him into the apartment, Allie peeked in the bag at the doughnuts. "Ooh, you are learning my weaknesses. Maybe, the police would like some."

He balked, jarring her to a halt with him. "I thought you were going to stay at my apartment."

She straightened her back and faced him. "I live here." She snatched the bag from him and strolled into the kitchen.

Josh followed close on her heels. Despite the firmness in her tone, her hand trembled when she reached for a coffee cup in the cupboard. He released an astonished, mirthless laugh. "I'm scared to death for you. Does that count?"

Allie spun around and faced him. "Oh, Josh." She closed the distance between them. "I had things to do," she said softly, touching his cheek.

"I asked you to—"

She raised her chin, stubbornly struggling for calm. "I know what you asked." Unwittingly a weariness slipped over her. "And I appreciate your concern." She swallowed the tightness in her throat. He would misunderstand. He would think that she was afraid. But it wasn't fear for her own safety that threatened to weaken her. It was confusion. "I have to lead my own life," she said as much for him as herself.

He counted to five. He knew he was overreacting, but dammit, did she have to be so obstinate? Tempted to shake some sense into her, he jammed his hands in his pockets and whirled away to keep from saying more than he should. All he'd asked was that she stay in his apartment. Asked. Hell, he'd appealed to her. He hadn't made any demands. He hadn't stifled her precious freedom.

Minutes seemed like hours before the police arrived. Allie went through a brief explanation to the police officers who'd answered her call, telling them about her previous complaint.

The younger one eyed the jimmied lock. "Someone wanted to get in bad."

"Obvious deduction," Josh muttered, struggling for patience. "What are you going to do about it?" As both men swung confused expressions back at him, Josh spoke slowly as if talking to small children. "To protect her."

"The police don't provide a protection agency for a possible break-in."

Before he exploded, Josh stormed into the kitchen.

While he paced, Allie answered the rest of the officers' questions. After seeing them out, she peeked into the kitchen. For only a second, her eyes made contact with Josh's. Though she saw less anger in them, he strode past her to the window, looked out and then strolled back to her. Allie watched him pace a path across the carpeting several times while she listened to her answering machine and the two messages—one from the radio station and the other from her sister. Marilyn's voice sounded more tense than usual. Allie flicked off the machine and dialed the radio station. When she finished, concerned for her sister, she dialed her number. Ten rings later, she gave up trying to reach her.

As she set down the receiver, Josh planted his feet. They would have it out now. She had to be reasonable. She had to stay at his apartment.

"Odd," she said suddenly. "My sister never calls me twice in such a short amount of time."

He drew a hard breath. If her thoughts were on someone else, nothing he said would be heard. "Maybe, she misses you."

In a gentling move, Allie rested a hand on his shoulder and leaned closer, pressing her forehead against his. "She's a busy woman. Too busy for idle chitchat. Even with a sister whom she might be missing."

"People change."

"I suppose they do," she said, stepping away.

He'd changed. He used to believe nothing mattered but his work and returning to Barrington to make a home for himself. Now, one woman came first in his thoughts always. At her flurry of movement, he looked back over his shoulder. "What's going on?"

Allie passed her lips across his before she snatched up her windbreaker. "I have to leave right away," she said with a glance at the clock. "Mr. Clements—the general manager at the radio station—asked if I'd come in early."

"I'll drive you," he insisted.

"You don't have to."

She'd taken only one step toward the door when he reached out and caught her at the waist, stopping her. Bringing her before him, he forced her to face him. "I have to, Allie."

"I—"

He shook his head. "Not for you. For me. Whether you need me to or not doesn't matter, I need to drive you. I need to know you're safe."

Neil cornered her five minutes after she arrived at the radio station.

"I can't talk now," Allie appealed. "Mr. Clements wants to see me."

"Think he heard about our deal?"

Allie frowned in confusion. "How could he? Anyway, why would that matter?"

"Some bosses like to fire you before you quit."

"Ray Clements doesn't seem like that sort of boss."

He shrugged. "Who knows. So, I'll call Los Angeles and tell them—"

Allie held up a halting hand. "Don't do that. We need to discuss this more," she insisted.

"What's to discuss?"

"I don't have the time right now," she said firmly.

He sighed heavily. "I don't see the problem, Allie. All you have to do is say yes."

How simple he made that sound. She strolled toward Ray Clements's office, wondering why she was having so much trouble saying that three-letter word. She should be thrilled with the offer. She should want to leave. She'd always looked forward to change before. Why was she hesitating now? Because of Josh?

On a sigh, she shook her head and drew a deep, relaxing breath against her own confusion before she raised a fist to rap on Ray Clements's door.

His gray head bent as she entered, he looked up, but he didn't smile. Never a good sign, Allie decided.

"Allie, thank you for coming in early." He bent his head to skim the log book. "According to Junior's scheduling, you're playing songs that aren't on it."

Allie took a long breath. "They were requests," she admitted, moving closer to his desk. "I know that I shouldn't have done that without Junior's okay, but—" She paused. "Frankly, people who talk to me sometimes request a song. To refuse them seems dumb. I thought it was better to play their requests."

He leaned back in the chair. "Ratings aren't doing too well. We tried a few promotional ideas, but I'm sure you know that they weren't highly successful."

As he gestured toward a chair, she sank on it.

"Demographic studies indicate we're not appealing to our audience. And let me tell you that the old man isn't happy. He's not happy with me or Junior. He's not happy with very much lately except you."

To say she wasn't stunned would have been lying. Though his words complimented her, she tensely clutched at the arms of the chair. "Me?"

"Yes. Your program is doing well even though you have the lowest listening audience at that time of the morning. How do you explain that?"

"I couldn't say."

"I think that it's because you listen to people. You're right. Playing their requests was an excellent idea. I've heard a great deal of good things about you. Previous station managers gave you excellent references. Your co-workers all like you."

Muddled and wondering where the conversation was going, she nervously shifted on the chair.

"I'd like you to take over Junior's position as Program Manager. You understand what the audience wants. We need that."

Allie caught herself gaping and shut her mouth.

A slip of a smile twitched his lips. "No response?"

"Shock," she admitted.

He belly-laughed. "I love doing that to people. Now, to save face, Junior will finish out the month, but then I'd like you to take over. You have the right qualities to make this radio station number one. Qualities I admire."

On shaky legs, Allie left his office. He'd given her time to make a decision. It was a step up in broadcasting. She was being offered more than a fly-by-night position. She was being offered an opportunity to start at the ground level and build the radio station into Barrington's finest. Anyone would be thrilled.

Somehow, she got through her program without making any obvious mistakes. But she had too much on her mind. Neil. The new job offer. The threats. Josh. And a faculty dinner, she thought on a sigh, wondering if she was crazy to have accepted.

She spent most of the next day struggling with indecision. She'd always thought that she didn't want to be tied to any job, any place, like everyone else in her family. She wanted the freedom to live her life without any demands. So why hadn't she said no to Ray? Why couldn't she make any decisions lately?

By five-thirty that evening, her most immediate problem was what she should wear. She stood before her closet and eyed a casual wardrobe, more filled with jeans and loose-fitting blouses than dresses with classic lines. The few dresses that she had were trendy: bright in color, unusual in style and definitely not conservative.

Go with what you've got, she mused, pulling out a multicolored, full-skirted dress that bared her shoulders.

Chapter Ten

She was a knockout. Josh noted the glances cast in their direction as they entered the roomful of people. She was a whisper of springtime in the midst of autumn stillness.

She was nervous, Allie realized. She wanted to make a good impression. She wanted the people she met to view her as perfect. How long had it been since she'd had such a thought? She was crazy to go with him. "You were crazy to ask me to come with you," she murmured.

He'd sensed her nervousness even before she'd announced it. "Be yourself." Reassuringly he placed a hand around the back of her neck and caressed it. "That's the woman I brought with me."

Several people stood near French doors, talking as if conspirators in some international plot. "She'll never fit into the mold for people like this," Allie quipped.

"Duplications are boring."

Allie sent him a weak smile. Everyone seemed so relaxed. She wished that she was. "I might giggle at the wrong time."

"You have a tendency to do that," he teased, finding her hand. "It's hard to be passionate when a woman giggles."

She laughed at his reminder of a previous day. "I've never tried to make love on a bed of crackers."

"You were the one who needed a snack," he reminded her.

"I was hungry."

"So was I."

She raised a smile to him. "I do remember."

"And that was a first for me."

A disbelieving expression knitted her brows. "A first?"

"I've never made love on a floor when a bed was so near."

Allie giggled then noted the people close by. "Shh," she cautioned.

"Let them hear." He kissed her cheek. "Then they'll know that I'm in love."

A shadow of concern fell across her face. *Don't be in love with me. I'll hurt you,* she wanted to say.

He sent her an appreciative look, his eyes sweeping down the cloth of the shiny multicolored dress. "You look very beautiful."

She'd heard similar compliments before. She'd never taken them to heart. Beauty meant nothing. Brains, achievements, success elicited admiration in the Gentry household. Compliments she'd received about her beauty had always fallen flat. They seemed so empty and shallow in comparison—until now. He made the compliment seem special. He made life seem different to her. "Thank you," she said softly. "Can I return the compliment?"

His head went back with soft laughter. "Never beautiful." He hooked her arm in his and urged her further into the room.

"Terrific?"

"I'll take terrific," he said before looking away in response to Nate's approach.

Nate's hands closed around Allie's in a welcoming handshake. "People are anxious to meet the broadcaster who's leading the campaign against ugly garbage cans."

Allie cringed inwardly.

Smiling, Josh touched the small of Allie's back. "Next week she has a different cause. Save the axolotls."

"I didn't know we had any here," Nate said, puzzled.

That he'd nearly parroted Josh's comment on the subject stirred Allie's laughter.

Josh admirably held onto a deadpan expression. "They're becoming extinct."

A seriousness crept into Nate's voice. "Then by all means, we should save them." He rolled his eyes in the direction of the couples nearby. "Shall we join the others?"

Josh curled a hand over Allie's shoulder. Beneath his fingers, he felt a tenseness that contradicted the smile firmly riveted to her face. "Stay clear of the stiff-looking woman perched on the straight back chair," he whispered in her ear.

Allie swung a look up at him. Was he afraid that she would embarrass him? Was that why he'd given her the warning?

"She clucks her tongue after every word," he added on a laugh.

"Clucking Corinne," Nate drolled as he strolled beside them.

Unfortunately, Allie learned firsthand that Corinne did cluck. Politely she listened to the woman's lengthy discussion about dramatists altering Greek tragedy.

Allie relied on years of training. Her family had expected a certain behavior. For Josh, she would mingle, offer polite inconsequential conversation with people who didn't care an iota about what she was saying.

Beside them, Nate treated her as if she were a longtime friend. Allie sensed that she could have had two heads and he and his wife would have accepted her.

"Let me introduce you to a few other people," Nate said, turning toward the couple beside him.

They were deep in discussion about literature but nodded hellos.

"Which play are they doing?" the woman asked, refocusing on the man beside her.

"*Titus Andronicus*," the man murmured in a dismal tone.

Someone standing nearby groaned at the mention of the play.

"My sentiments, too," another woman injected before staring curiously at Allie.

The moment Josh made the introduction to Harriet Forsythe, the dean's wife, a cowardly streak slithered through Allie. The petite, white-haired woman before her was important to Josh.

The woman's eyes narrowed inquisitively. "I've been told that you work at one of the radio stations."

Here it comes, Allie thought. That slight inflection in the voice or that look of disdain.

"Being a deejay sounds like such interesting work. I don't know how you manage to keep talking without your voice giving out. I recall the days when my husband lectured. He always was certain that he'd never talk again. Do you have a secret?"

With one smiling question, the woman was offering a friendliness that Allie hadn't expected. Feeling less awkward, she matched the woman's smile, "Commercials."

"Perhaps, professors should have such breaks." Harriet gave her a thoughtful look. "I read that deejays are the next best things to psychiatrists. Is there any truth to that?"

Allie accepted her interest as genuine. "To a point. Listeners begin to think of deejays as their friends. A couple of times a week, I get calls from people who just want to talk about their divorce or their kids or a problem that they have."

"And you talk to them?"

"Of course. They wouldn't have called if they hadn't needed someone. If I can be that person, then why not? I don't offer advice. They're not calling for it. They simply need someone to listen to them."

Harriet suddenly wagged a finger at her. "Now, I recall where I've seen you before. When we were introduced, I thought you looked familiar. You visit the children's hospital every week, don't you?"

Wondering where the conversation was headed, Allie offered a hesitant nod.

Harriet's face brightened. "I often go there myself." Her hand touched Allie's arm affectionately. "You're the one who brought in that enormous stuffed giraffe for one of the children. In fact, if I have the story right, you buy a different stuffed animal every week for one of the children."

"They appreciate little things."

"I'd say that caring about someone else isn't so unimportant."

The briefest flicker of a question flashed across Josh's face before he bent his head to whisper in Allie's ear. "Someone should wash your mouth out with soap for fibbing."

Allie grinned up at him. "You believed me, didn't you?"

He couldn't deny that he'd expected a silliness from her. She'd probably had a silent laugh at his expense when she'd told him the giraffe was her new pet. Looking back, he couldn't blame her for doubting his feelings for her. He'd acted like a stuffed shirt when they'd met, reacting predictably to even the slightest oddities. The realization wasn't a comfortable one. Needing a moment alone with his own thoughts, he squeezed her waist to steal her attention. The eyes that turned up to him danced with their usual warmth. "Would you like a drink?"

"A white wine."

He heard the familiar huskiness that slid into her voice when her mood was lighthearted. "I'll be only a moment."

As he stepped away, Nate inched closer to Allie. "Did you know that I attempted to play matchmaker for Josh?" he asked Allie.

Harriet's lips curved upward in a slip of a smile. "With all of the usual single women around the campus who have the right credentials."

"Josh halfheartedly went along with the idea," Nate said with a glance at Allie. "For a little while. But my prearranged dates failed. He hadn't any list of qualifications, so I was guessing blindly. If he'd had some, I might have done better."

Allie managed a semblance of a smile though she found herself gritting her teeth. "Well, perhaps you'll find someone soon for him who's compatible."

Nate's eyes sparkled with humor. "He seems quite capable of finding the person he wanted without any help from any of us."

Her brows arching, Harriet responded without a blink of an eye, "An obvious deduction, Nathaniel."

As he lightly, reassuringly touched her back, Allie turned away in confusion. They couldn't believe that *she* was right for Josh?

"Do you play?" Harriet asked, following Allie's gaze and obviously believing she was eyeing the piano.

Allie felt her stomach somersault.

"Yes, she does," Nate offered helpfully. "Josh told me something about Julliard."

"Oh, really?"

All of Allie's childhood inadequacies threatened to surge forward. Tension coiled around her like a tight spring. She wouldn't shrink, she told herself. She was a grown woman. Unlike then, she had choices now. She didn't have to play if she didn't want to.

"Herbert likes Beethoven," Harriet said about her husband. "I tell you that because most of the professors and their companions try hard to please my husband." She sent Nate a knowing smile. "Isn't that true?" she asked. "Academia is no different than business. Office politics, my dear," she said, turning back to Allie, "are always a part of life."

Allie drew a hard breath. She wasn't the corporate wife type. Innocently she could do something and destroy everything Josh had worked for.

"I'd really enjoy listening to you play something," Harriet urged.

Visually Allie searched for Josh. Carrying wine glasses, he was winding his way back to her. She couldn't change for him. She'd never been suited for the quiet, dignified world before. That's what he hadn't acknowledged as he'd nudged her toward a lifestyle that she'd vowed to avoid. It was time he realized what she'd always known. She wouldn't fit in. "I prefer to play ragtime," she said.

Harriet cast an askance glance at the piano. "Wouldn't that be a nice change of pace."

Allie wasn't sure if the woman's comment was genuine or not.

"Would you play for us?"

She would play, Allie decided as she moved on wooden legs toward the piano. Because playing had always been a private joy for her, as the music danced in the air she forgot everything except her delight in playing. The conversation, the clink of ice cubes in glasses, the feeling of being watched and judged slipped away.

Standing beside Josh, Nate peered over the rim of his glasses at him. "A lovely woman. I can understand why you're so taken with her."

Josh reached for a cracker from the buffet table. "Can you?"

"Oh, yes. When she enters a room so does sunshine."

Around them, the crowd quieted as she played a Scott Joplin ragtime tune. The music was like her. Bright. Light-spirited. Energetic. She was full of surprises. Intelligent, talented, strong-minded, compassionate, she hid behind a fluffy image. "It is more than that," he said with certainty.

"I assumed it was."

"And she doesn't want any part of this," he said with a sweep of his arm.

His eyes on Allie, Nate frowned. "Why not?"

"It reeks of proper. Of too much discipline. Or whatever she thinks might place too much restraint on her."

"Restraint?" He looked even more baffled.

"She's like a butterfly."

Understanding swept into Nate's voice. "You'll convince her that we're not so bad."

Josh snorted.

The older man's frown deepened. "And you obviously can't walk away."

"I won't have to," Josh shrugged. "She'll eventually fly away."

"I must say this isn't an easy problem." He patted Josh's shoulder. "But if anyone can solve it, you will."

Josh wished that he had as much confidence in himself. Whether she liked the idea or not, he did love her. His biggest problem at the moment was convincing her that she felt the same about him. He thought of ways to approach her about marriage. Cajole, tease, demand. None of them seemed like a winning one. He only knew he wouldn't let go of her without a fight. Time might be the key. If she took that job in Los Angeles, she would be gone from his life. He had only so much time to convince her that they were meant for each other.

He wound his way past people to reach her. Every moment with her unveiled something new to him about her. Every moment made him ache for an eternity with her.

"You're modest," he said later, during a moment alone with her. As she sent him a baffled look, he noted her white-knuckled grip on the stem of her wineglass. "On the ivories." Setting a hand on her bare shoulder, he inched her closer. "You're very good."

"Not really." She sipped the wine he'd handed her. "I attempted to be a concert pianist. But I deserted that idea of a career after insufferable days of never pleasing a music teacher."

Recalling his mother's patience with her students, he wondered who was really at fault. "One teacher. Teachers aren't infallible. Some are good. Some are bad. He—"

"She," Allie corrected.

"She might have been—"

"She was one of many who all shook their heads as if I had a terminal disease. She'd tell me to practice, and I'd be outside daydreaming in the sunshine. But I loved music, in any form. I needed a life to revolve around it. That's why I became a deejay."

Instinctively he curled a hand tighter on her shoulder as her rambling revealed how nervous she really was.

"I started working as a clerk, filing musical tapes. One day, a deejay couldn't get to work because of flooding, and I got my break."

Josh believed more than luck played a part in the direction she'd taken. Through dinner, she charmed anyone she met. Her eyes sparkled with merriment in response to a colleague's story about the football player who dressed his girlfriend in his clothes, including football pads, to take an exam for him.

As Professor Tuborn cut in and told a tale of woe about his schedule, those same eyes grew serious with interest. She listened intently. She had a knack for it, for making people feel important. Laughingly she talked to a visiting professor, whipping back responses in fluent French. She lied to herself, Josh thought. She belonged anywhere that she chose.

With an announcement of coffee and after-dinner liqueurs, Josh ushered Allie toward the living room again. Nothing she'd expected was true. She'd anticipated lengthy, boring discussions; snooty looks; phony smiles. She'd attended dozens of dinners at home filled with game playing and power struggles. But she was treated instead to a congenial debate about snowmobiles and a discussion about reinstating the annual bonfire at the college on Halloween night.

She no longer felt a stiff awkwardness, but before they could join the others in the room, an anxiousness for Josh edged forward. With her peripheral vision, she caught sight of Dean Forsythe carving a path toward them. Had this been the evening when the chairmanship would be announced? Nervous for Josh, she squeezed his arm and rushed an excuse to leave his side before the man reached them.

Questioningly Josh looked down at her. For a second, her eyes met his. A message of good luck stretched to him without a word spoken. Until that moment, he hadn't realized that he'd forgotten to tell her about the chairmanship. Watching her, he smiled at himself, aware that something so important weeks ago had entirely tumbled from his mind until that moment.

"Have you seen Tuborn, Josh?" A hint of tiredness accompanied the Dean's question. "I understand his nose is out-of-joint about the seating arrangement at dinner."

Josh responded with a grin. "He's in the other room."

"I'd better find him. I hope you're enjoying yourself."

"I am," Josh said easily while scanning the sea of faces for Allie.

"About your companion—"

Josh met his gaze.

"My wife is quite taken with her. It's been a pleasure meeting her."

Holding her breath, Allie followed Josh's progress across the room to her. His expression told her nothing. "Good news?" she asked when he stopped beside her and rested his hand on the small of her back.

Distractedly watching Tuborn sulking in a corner, he answered with a shake of his head. "No, I didn't get the chairmanship."

A weightiness bore down on her. "Oh, Josh—" Was she responsible? If he hadn't brought her would— "I tried to warn you," she said softly.

The concern in her voice snapped his attention back to her. "Warn me about what?" His own puzzlement lasted only for a second.

Allie fought to bring words forward. "I hurt your chances, didn't I?"

The worry on her face tugged at his heart. "Oh, Allie." With a fingertip, he tilted her face up to his. "I was told yesterday, but I forgot to tell you. Everyone here thinks you're delightful."

Delightful? She glanced around her. Hadn't she dressed wrong? Hadn't she laughed too loudly, talked too much? Hadn't she had a good time? she realized suddenly.

Lightly he pressed his lips to hers, not caring who was watching. "I'd like time alone with you before you leave for the radio station. Let's go home now."

Despite his reassurance, she fought old doubts while they drove toward home. "Tell me now what happened with Dean Forsythe."

"He had a list of logical reasons why I was wrong for the position."

"Logical to him only. Or to you, too?"

"I understood."

She shifted on the seat and searched his face for his true feelings. Shadows emphasized the hard angles and the hollows of his face.

"I would have liked it," he admitted with a dismissing shrug. "But I'll get it eventually."

So sure of himself. So confident. She'd never known that. "If it's what you want, I hope you do."

He was used to waiting for things. In a few years, he would have what he'd worked hard for professionally. But would he have her? he wondered as he pulled up to the curb and flicked off the ignition.

Allie pushed open her door and waited for him. "Everyone was nice." She responded to his lopsided grin and snuggled closer. "I had a wonderful time. But then I liked Nate and Edith immediately. And the Dean's wife—Harriet," she corrected, "she and I share a mutual interest." With a token of disbelief, she shook her head as they strolled toward the apartment building. "I would never have expected her to like Spike Jones records."

"Neither would I," he admitted, tightening his arm around her waist.

As she walked so close to him that her hip brushed his, she felt the slight shift of his body when he looked to the side. Even beneath the moonlight, she could see his disapproving scowl. "You're frowning again," she teased.

Laughter at himself crept into his voice as he continued to stare at a pile of raked leaves. "I was thinking that someone wasted a lot of time." At her quizzical expression, he gestured toward the tree and the leaves fluttering away.

"Could be that they just enjoyed doing it," she responded. At every turn, the differences between them sprang forward. She might do something just for enjoyment. Everything he did had a purpose.

He shot a glance down at her and grinned self-deprecatingly. "I'm being too serious again, huh?"

"A little."

He accepted the tease in her voice.

"*I* prefer to play in them." She set her head on his shoulder and stared up at a pale autumn moon. Heavy pewter clouds carpeted the sky. The wind wailed with a soft crooning sound as if warning them of an impending harshness. Leaves rustled beneath the wind's blustery breath and scurried across the street. The elements for a brisk autumn night surrounded her yet she felt the warmth of a summer's evening. "Want to roll in them with me?"

His chuckle rippled in the silent air. "I'd rather roll on the bed." At her feigned comical scowl, his laugh accompanied them up the stairs. "You need to perfect that glare," he teased.

She sighed resignedly. "I guess I'll stick to winking."

He curled an arm around her waist. "Good idea. I've grown fond of your twitch."

When he pushed the door open, she preceded him into the apartment. "Is winking a talent?" she asked on a weak smile.

Before she could move away, he caught her at the waist and pulled her back to him. "You have many talents."

"Not really."

He smiled wryly. "You just won't see yourself clearly. Does bright and energetic count?"

She pulled back to ease from him but he held firm.

"Not everyone knows how to listen and make people feel important, Allie."

On a sigh at his stubbornness, she slipped away and shrugged off her coat. "You're not trying to understand. I'm—"

"A lovely woman."

Allie raised her chin a notch. "My sisters are beautiful."

"But are they lovely?"

She frowned as he closed the inches between them.

"Not just lovely to look at." Lightly he pressed a finger to her chest. "In here. You're beautiful. Here, too," he said softly, framing her face with his hands.

Emotion flooded her. He accepted so much about her, so many of the quirks that other people had always wagged their heads in exasperation at. He made her feel wanted. Loved. She longed to cling and believe in something as fragile as love.

"They couldn't possibly be," he whispered in a voice more hoarse than usual before his mouth closed over hers again.

With a kiss that was hard, a kiss meant to linger forever in her memory, a kiss meant to make the ache for him never disappear, he linked her to him. Distance wouldn't matter. She would never forget these moments—this moment. And closing her eyes, she gave in to everything she'd tried to deny. Her heart was already bound to the one racing with her own.

Sliding her hands up his back, she pulled him close, needing more than something as simplistic as a physical nearness. Want was easy to deny. Need was different. Need meant an intimacy that she'd vowed never to accept. But she couldn't think when with him. At the caress of his hand trailing down her back, skimming the length of her thigh, she covered his face with slow, nibbling kisses.

The languid pace lasted less than a minute. The hunger, the headiness, the heat swamped her. She heard his deep moan, felt his arousal and strained against him. Wild, she sought the flesh beneath his clothes, yearned for the slick texture of his damp skin on her.

With the same quickness that he slid clothes from her, she undressed him. As if it were the first time, all fire and heat, they pushed aside gentleness. A storm gathered around them with an intoxicating force that swayed her against him.

Desire drugged her before she could grab her next breath. She surrendered to its exhilaration and took her fill of the lips smothering hers. As he rushed her, she hurried him until only sensations mattered. Softly, he murmured her name while he skimmed her body with his hands and mouth. She felt no patience in him. Within a heartbeat, with the flick of his tongue, he led her on a breathless journey that tantalized and teased and demanded response.

Tense beneath a desperate urgency, she glided her tongue across his chest and down his stomach. She matched his intensity, her mouth playing across his flesh as if she would never know his taste again, and as she lowered her head, all her thoughts centered on pleasing him. She tasted and touched, marveling at the ripple of muscles beneath her lips, the saltiness on her tongue.

They drove each other. As she sighed, he groaned. As she trembled, he shuddered, and still she strained to bind him even closer to her, flattening her body to his as if trying to blend the warmth and dampness of their flesh.

No more whispery caresses, no more gentle strokes. She returned his challenge even as she submitted. She blocked out everything—all the doubts and all the fears. When she was with him, she felt none of them. Only feelings mattered as every breath drawn, every sound uttered, every beat of her pulse was for him. She was consumed by more than desire's pleasure, more than its obsessing ache. Even as she tried to resist and ignore it, one emotion—love—persisted, filling her, surpassing the fleeting simplicity of passion, and binding her to him.

He couldn't say when her delicate hands sent him scrambling to grasp the edge of reason. He was beyond thinking. Her heart pounding against his echoed the sound of his own. He stopped breathing, his body quivering in anticipation when she sat up on her knees. With his hands on her hips, he guided her, pulling her closer, never letting her eyes leave his. Raw emotions overwhelmed him as she arched above him, her paleness washed in the glow of early moonlight. She snatched every breath she could draw from him. As if this moment were their last, she gave him everything, more than he'd ever expected, and something close to fear coiled within him. It vanished before he could acknowledge it, as he spun beneath the inevitable senselessness, and then nothing else mattered but the heat.

On a heady sigh, on a breath, he whispered her name as a fire leaped through him, spreading with a quickness that left him gasping. Mindless to everything but his need for her, he succumbed to the swift pang of desire wrenching him.

Head back, eyes closed, he relinquished it to her willingly, eagerly. On a moan, he shuddered with a pleasure that exceeded any he'd ever known. For a few moments, he knew wherever she wanted to go, wherever she drifted, he would follow. Nothing mattered but being with her—not for just these moments—but for an eternity.

Chapter Eleven

At the brush of Allie's fingers over his chest, Josh groped his way back to reality. "Hungry?"

"Crackers and cheese," she said on a laugh.

He smiled, tugging her closer. "And a bottle of wine."

"Does a well-prepared professor have all that?"

"Nope, you ate all the crackers the last time."

Allie nipped at his shoulder. "Then I guess we'll have to think of something else."

"Anything you want," he murmured against her hair.

"I'd like—"

She stiffened beside him at the jarring shrill of the phone.

"Damn," he mumbled the word and reached back, fumbling to stop the sound. Beside him, Allie lay so still in wary anticipation that he wondered if she were breathing. In the dimness of the room, his eyes locked with hers as he offered the receiver to her. She looked pale and frightened. "Do you want me to answer it?" he asked, not knowing of any other way to ease the emotion for her.

How easy it would be to say yes, she realized, but she couldn't allow someone to sweep so much fear into her life that she was afraid to answer her own phone. In a jerky, hesitant move, she accepted the receiver from him and managed a barely audible, "Hello."

"Allison, it's Mother."

Allie squeezed her eyes tight, willing herself to keep a control, even a tenuous one, on emotions. "Mother," she said on a relieved sigh.

Satisfied that it wasn't another silent call, he produced a slim smile because she seemed to need it. With a thumb, he smoothed hair away from her cheek and kissed it. "I'll be back to drive you to work," he whispered, sliding from the bed.

Allie nodded a response and drew a long, relaxing breath, wishing she could pull him back to her, forget the phone call, forget work, forget everything but him.

"Have you talked to your sister recently?"

She snapped her mind back to the phone call. If she rushed conversation, her mother would remind her, as she'd often done, about the necessity to allot time properly. An old argument. One that Allie didn't feel up to. "I haven't heard from Sarah in months," she managed in an even voice. "Marilyn called twice in the past week."

"I assumed that Marilyn would feel compelled to call you."

Crawling out of the bed, Allie frowned in puzzlement.

"Don't you have anything to say?"

Allie considered the odd phrasing of her mother's question. What was it that she should be saying that she wasn't? What faux pas was she committing this time? she wondered while yanking a blue sweatshirt over her head.

"About your sister—"

Allie focused on her mother's voice again. "Marilyn?"

"Of course, Marilyn. She, more than Sarah, has always been as changeable as the weather."

"And I was—"

"Like a butterfly." Her mother attempted a hint of humor. "But you were always predictable."

Allie pulled back from the phone with a frown. She wasn't predictable. Had she been distant from her mother for so long that she'd forgotten? This once, she didn't feel like playing word games just for the sake of keeping peace. "What do you mean?"

"Whatever I said was black, you undoubtedly decided it was white. I could always depend on that. Marilyn, on the other hand, is sweet as springtime one moment and as turbulent as a tropical storm the next."

Confused by the conversation that seemed to have no definite purpose, Allie waited, hoping her mother's next words would explain her uncharacteristic chattiness.

"I was certain that you'd hear from her." Her voice edged with disapproval. "She's considering a divorce."

Allie cradled the phone between her jaw and shoulder while she tugged on jeans.

"I never realized that Marilyn was so unhappy with him."

"Has she filed for a divorce yet?" Allie asked, wiggling her toes into a shoe.

"No, of course not," her mother said firmly.

"But if she's—"

"Allison, think."

Allie cringed at the familiar reprimand.

"I said that she was considering a divorce. She can't divorce him. She'd jeopardize too much."

"Jeopardize what?" On hands and knees, she hunted under the bed for the second shoe.

"Hartwell and Handel is a prestigious, conservative law firm. Its clients include large corporations. Corporations that assume that the lawyers at the firm are steady and dependable. What would they think if they heard that two of the firm's lawyers couldn't manage their own marriage? *I* certainly would wonder about the professional ability of someone who couldn't manage their personal life better."

"But if she isn't happy—"

"Happiness comes in many forms."

Of course, their careers wouldn't be risked. Sitting back on her heels with the shoe dangling from her fingers, she sighed at the lengthy explanation and glanced at the clock. "So she'll stay with him?" she asked as she plopped back against the footboard of the bed and shoved her foot into the second sneaker.

"I suggest we convince her that would be wise. I expect you'll offer that advice if she calls."

Without warning, a tension at the base of her skull tightened like a vise. During the past few weeks, despite the underlying fear popping into her life, she'd felt happy. Happy enough that she'd forgotten so many of the pressures and demands that she'd left behind.

"Allison, you will do that, won't you?"

"I'll talk to her," she answered to end the conversation quickly.

"Before you leave, I suppose I should tell you the rest of the news. Your father is in Brazil now, researching primates. And he's seeing some woman who's the same age as Marilyn," she added as an afterthought. "Then—well—who knows where he'll move to. Like you, he's hard to keep track of. Today, you're in Vermont and tomorrow only you know where you'll want to go."

Because too many thoughts were rushing through her mind, Allie hurried words. "California, maybe."

"I see. Another job?"

"Yes," Allie answered. "A morning slot."

"Is that good?"

"It could be."

"When are you moving?"

Allie froze with the question. "When?" All this time, she'd never allowed herself to think about the actual move, to make it a fact. "I—"

As if she'd given an affirmative response, her mother released what sounded like a long-suffering sigh. "Soon, I suppose. As you always told me, you know what's best for yourself," she responded. "You always seemed to in the past."

Allie frowned at the hint of a compliment.

"I always tried to help you as I did your sisters, but you were always your own person." A tight smile edged her mother's voice. "You never required mine or your father's help in the way that your sisters did. Even now. Look at your sisters." Her voice filled with exasperation. "They're so dissatisfied. And I do feel badly for Marilyn."

"Me, too," Allie admitted honestly, but she suddenly felt sad for herself, too. And she didn't know why.

Josh waited at her bedroom door for her. He'd watched emotions flicker across her face—discomfort, disbelief, and then sadness. She looked pale even as she set down the receiver. "Is something wrong?"

At the shake of her head, he felt his heart tighten.

There was so much she wanted to say, but how could she explain what she didn't understand? She'd never wanted to get too close to him. Even with intimacy, she'd told herself that she wouldn't get involved with him. She'd led such an uncomplicated life for the past five years, a life free of tense moments because she'd kept her distance from closeness with anyone. And through those years, she'd never disappointed anyone, because she'd made no promises to anyone but herself. During the time with Josh, she'd nearly forgotten all those promises. One phone call, she realized. All she'd needed was one phone call to remind her of what she didn't want in her life again.

Too quiet, Josh reflected. She was too damn quiet to suit him. As he drove her to the radio station, he longed for sunshine even as he stared out at the darkness of night. He longed to say words. Ironically they were simple words, yet the most difficult he'd ever wanted to say.

As he zipped the car into the parking lot adjacent to the radio station, he told himself not to rush her. She seemed tenser than usual, her back straight, her hands tight on the straps of her purse. The sight of her so uptight made him anxious, more anxious than he wanted to be. "What's happening with that Los Angeles deal?"

Allie darted an apprehensive glance at him. "Nothing is firm yet." Crowded by emotions for her family, for him, she felt entangled in a web of indecision. Life had seemed so simple weeks ago. Why had it grown so complicated? Why did she feel as if the car was shrinking, as if the threat of being smothered was only a breath away? "Management wants me to do something else. They've offered me the position of program director."

Because her expression remained serious, Josh stifled an urge to congratulate her. His own edginess intensified. With the same easy flicking motion that he turned off the ignition, he felt her slipping away from him. Her lingering silence detonated a warning in his brain and he heard the distinct ticking as if a countdown had begun before an explosion. "And?" he asked simply because he couldn't make himself say more.

She couldn't help the feeling building within her. With him, her life would be the same again. She would have gone full circle. She would have to conform to others' rules. She'd be expected to dress differently. She'd see the same people day in and day out. A staidness would settle over her and demands for her to do certain things would increase. "And Neil needs an answer about the Los Angeles offer. It's a great opportunity. I should have told him sooner." She forced herself to shed a coward's coat. "I should have told you," she said, avoiding his eyes.

"Told me what?"

"I'll be leaving."

One second. Two. Maybe, only three passed, but they seemed like eternity. He drew a hard breath. Why hadn't he ever prepared himself for those words? "What about us?" he asked as an ache swelled within him to bridge the distance between them and yank her to him.

She struggled to ignore the hurt in his voice. "I never planned to stay." Her words came out strangled as feelings for him made her want to give in to something that she'd sworn she'd stay clear of. "I never meant for any of this to happen."

When she started to turn her face away, he grabbed her arm, stopping her, forcing her to look at him. "I need a lot of other things in my life. One of them is you."

She shook her head. "I'm not what you need. I'm not the right woman for a professor."

"We're not talking about my occupation. We're talking about you and me."

She couldn't handle this now. She sensed what he wanted to hear from her, but she couldn't give him what he wanted. "You need some woman who wants what you do. I'm not her, Josh." Caught up in a need to protect herself, she looked to the side and grabbed at the door handle as she spoke without thought. "Your life is too rigid for me."

"A lame reason."

She swung a look back at him. "The truth."

"No, it isn't. You won't be truthful with yourself, or you'd admit what you really feel." He fought his own desperation. He wanted to beg her to stay. Pride wouldn't allow it. "Even if some man was willing to give up everything for you and traipse around the country with you like some gypsy, you'd find another reason to pull away. Who I am and what you think I am isn't the reason. It isn't my so-called rigid life-style. It isn't staying in one place that scares you. And it damn well has nothing to do with freedom."

"Then what is it?" Her chin lifted to a challenging angle for only a second. She saw his mouth tighten. She saw too much hurt in his eyes—too much pain—and her heart rolled over.

"Yourself. Ask yourself why you need to keep moving around."

"I like seeing—"

His hand slashed at the air. He ached inside. It wasn't something he would allow himself to think about now. "Forget it," he cut in sharply.

She tensed, fighting an urge to retreat. She thought him a quiet, reserved man. She'd seen him caught up in the heat of passion but never in the blaze of anger. She saw an intensity in his eyes that frightened her and rippled a pain she'd never felt before through her. Was this love? she wondered. God, it hurt. She didn't want to hurt him; she didn't want to be hurt. She loved him, she realized. She loved him so much she was afraid to stay with him. The thought seemed ridiculous, but until her mother's phone call, she'd allowed herself to forget that she'd come from a family where love hadn't existed, where no one had understood it. Even now, she wasn't sure her life would be any different from theirs. Hadn't she even chosen the kind of man they'd think of as perfect? "There's more to this than that," she said as she remembered one vital fact. Marriages never lasted in her family. "I promised myself that I'd never settle down, I'd never—"

Angrily he cut her off. "Dammit, don't!"

Her back stiffened. "Why are you doing this?"

"Doing what?"

"Pressuring me," she snapped.

On a mirthless laugh, he whipped his head away, furious that she had to ask the question. Wasn't love obvious?

"Being under pressure is something I went through most of my life. I won't go through it again. You're exactly the kind of man that they'd like me to get involved with. You're—"

He turned and looked at her slowly. "So you won't. Is that it? I'm too much like what they'd expect?" he shot back.

She stared into eyes filled with fury.

"Against all odds, you found yourself falling in love with someone they'd approve of, didn't you?"

"Stop it! You don't understand."

"Do you care at all about me?"

She stared blankly at him, struggling to breathe evenly as a weakness stormed her, threatening tears.

"If you love me—" A paleness swept over her face, stopping him.

On a long breath, Allie closed her eyes. He didn't realize that those were the worst words he could say to her. How many times had someone in her family used those words to manipulate or pressure her? If you love us, you'll go to Julliard. If you love us, you'll think about what marriage to Kyle will mean to yourself, to all of us. If you love us, you'll give up drifting around the country and get a real job. Because even breathing hurt, she couldn't manage more than a shake of her head.

"Do you even know what you want?" He fought the urge to grab her as she flung open the car door.

In the darkness of the car, he stared at her for a long, silent moment as if waiting. Allie gave him the only answer she could. "Freedom," she whispered.

As she slammed the car door and raced toward the building, she realized there was nothing more that she could say. Never in her life had she deliberately hurt anyone. Why did it have to be him? Why did she feel like crying? Why was he so important to her? For years, she hadn't allowed herself to feel so much for anyone.

Rushing into the radio station, she felt her heart lurch with misgivings. Had she made a mistake? Why did that thought suddenly haunt her? She'd never regretted leaving anywhere, anyone, before. She wanted to leave, didn't she? She'd never planned to stay. She would go to a new place and she'd forget, she told herself. As a twinge of doubt touched her heart, she swallowed hard against the knot in her throat.

The bite of the autumn wind still chilled her face as she entered the warmth of the building. And one thought lingered. What if she couldn't forget him?

Josh waited until she was inside the building. Outside the car, the wind howled. Inside, silence hung in the air. Irrationally a pain pierced him that seemed so real he winced. The need for her was agonizing, encompassing everything in his life. Didn't the car even seem darker since she'd left? Or was that his imagination?

He'd handled the moment all wrong. So caught up in his own uneasiness, he'd rushed her. But how could she walk away so easily? He couldn't walk away from her.

On a shake of his head, he flicked on the ignition. He was a fool. He'd always known that she would leave. She'd never played unfair with him. If he was hurting, it was his own damn fault. He'd forgotten that she was like the wind—light and airy, rushing, eager to go to someplace new.

All the rational thinking didn't help. He drove home as if being pursued by crazed men. Tension knotting his stomach, he gave himself no time to think once he parked his car. Immediately he took off, running as if his only hope existed in his total exhaustion. He challenged himself until muscles burned to the point of cramping.

As he strode back into the apartment, like a two-edged sword, he hated her at the moment as much as he loved her.

With the back of his hand, he wiped sweat from his face and plopped on the chair in his living room. Now what? he wondered, wishing he could analyze the problem. But love didn't fit into any logical slot, and all the education and all the experience in the world wouldn't help him reach a solution.

Briefly he toyed with the idea of going back to the radio station, but pride kept his backside planted to the chair.

Cradling a coffee cup in his hand, he stared across the room at the lithograph of the Rhine River. After Allie had discarded it, he'd retrieved it from the garbage. He'd thought then how different she was from him. They didn't like similar things. They had different ideas about their future. They would never belong together.

Now, he knew differently. The differences had made their time together interesting, not combative. They *did* belong together. But how the hell would he convince her of that? He couldn't force her to stay. And he couldn't make her admit that she loved him.

An ache buried itself within him. Setting down the coffee cup, he swore softly and then ran a hand across tired eyes. Needing a diversion from his own thoughts, he pulled out a stack of papers from one of his classes.

Allie waited to flick a switch on the console in the broadcasting booth. As Rod Stewart's raspy voice stretched for the final notes of a song, she hit the switch and began reading a commercial for a new shampoo. With another flick, she switched on the sponsor's prerecorded jingle about glossy hair with more body.

Straight ahead of her, behind glass was the dark office of Bill Vannen, Jr. At nine-thirty in the evening, a silence rang a music of its own through the darkened halls and offices of the radio station. The radio station was deserted now. Neil had handed her the microphone with a goodnight, Junior had waved in passing and Ray had ducked his head into the broadcasting booth to remind her that they had a new sponsor. Chad had tailed Ray toward the exit. Though she hadn't heard the distinct echo of the exit door closing, she'd felt the quietness around her.

The ticking of the clock filled her ears. Time speeding away. Time never standing still. She'd never cared before. But when all the time was gone for her, would she look back with regrets? Hours seemed to pass, but only minutes had ticked by.

Every creak unsettled her. She'd never minded the solitude before. Was she feeling more alone because of her argument with Josh? She squeezed her eyes tight in anguish. Why did she yearn to hear his voice? Why did the idea of leaving suddenly seem wrong? With a deep shuddering breath, she pressed her palms to her eyes. Flooded with emotions, she tried logical thinking. Eventually she would disappoint Josh. He would expect something of her that she'd fail to give him. But she already had, hadn't she? she thought, a moan escaping her lips. And why had she? He'd never tried to change her. He'd accepted everything about her. He'd only asked for one thing. Love.

A numbness floated over her so close to grief that her heart agonized at the emptiness. She fought the pain and the panic, knowing she didn't dare give in to it. With a mental shake of her head, she noted the time on the clock at the far wall. Alerted by the last few notes of the jingle, she leaned closer to the microphone to begin the commercial for a fast food restaurant. She announced the time and followed the commercial with a soft sell about tickets for the symphony's performances then flicked on the next song.

Standing, she stretched, wishing the time would tick by faster. She glanced toward the hallway. She couldn't hear anything beyond the soundproof broadcasting booth, but the sense of being watched chilled her.

Locked doors were a poor excuse for security, she thought as she stepped into the hallway. With a plastic ID card, anyone could get in. She knew, because she'd forgotten her key and had entered that way. Talk around the station included hiring a night watchman. Though all the doors were locked, Allie felt as if she weren't alone. She tried to slough aside her skittishness, but too many things had happened recently.

If she were smart, she would skip another cup of coffee. She would— She tensed at a sound—the distinct one of footsteps. As if the slightest breath might be heard, she held hers and listened for a moment longer. She heard nothing.

Was her imagination running wild? she wondered. She glanced back at the clock in the broadcasting room then retraced her steps and slid a prerecorded program into position. If she didn't make it back in time, the previous program would take over. There was nothing worse than dead airtime.

Closing the broadcasting booth door behind her, she edged around the corner cautiously. This was dumb, she thought. Whenever she'd watched a movie and had seen some Gothic heroine creeping up the steps with her candle, Allie had groaned at her stupidity. So what was she doing? Acting just as dimwitted.

Stopping in her tracks, she decided to return to the broadcasting booth. Either she would call the police or steady her nerves and excuse what she'd heard to a vivid imagination. She wasn't going to keep wandering around the radio station while a prerecorded show bored her listeners.

She took one step and froze as a shadow flickered across the hallway. Thin, lanky, it looked like a silhouette of Chad.

Allie stifled a breath and plastered her back to the wall. He had no business being at the radio station. She'd learned that he'd lied before about working extra hours. And because he wasn't issued a key, he had to have broken his way in. Why he had was the question Allie didn't want to ask herself.

She waited only until his shadow disappeared. On the toes of her sneakers, she raced in the opposite direction of the broadcasting booth and toward her office, toward a phone.

On a curse, Josh dropped the stack of student papers on the coffee table. No doubt Lincoln was turning over in his grave at some of the interpretations Josh had read of the Gettysburg Address.

With a shift of his body, he reached back and fiddled with the dial on the radio. For now, he needed to hear her voice. Later, he would go to the radio station. They'd talk again.

"You are listening to KFKQ and Allie Gentry with night music for lovers. This a favorite one of Mr. and Mrs. Peter Vanovitch. Lionel Ritchie's 'Endless Love.' Happy anniversary Mr. and Mrs. V."

The pen in Josh's hand slipped from his fingers and clattered on the desk. The Vanovitchs' anniversary was weeks ago. She'd dedicated that song to them then. Allie wouldn't be playing a tape of a program from weeks ago unless she was in trouble. In three strides, he was at the door, his heart racing with worry for her.

Chapter Twelve

She would have no reason to play a previous program unless—Josh fought thoughts from forming while he sped toward the radio station. He tried not to remember all the threats, but they no longer seemed like empty ones. A flood of cold fury surging through him, he felt numb as he whipped the car into the parking lot.

Police cars were everywhere, parked in helter-skelter fashion. Josh lunged for the door and flung it open. One step in, he faced a blue uniform.

"Where do you think you're going?"

The cop blocked his path to the stairs but not his view. At the clatter of footsteps, Josh broke the combative stare with the man before him. Looking past him, he saw Ray Clements standing on the landing.

"Where is she?" Josh yelled, his shoulder bumping the officer's as he took a step to the side.

"Let him up," Ray called out.

"Allie? Where is she—" He cut his words short. Looking pale, her slim hand tight on the banister, she descended the steps and then stopped on the landing beside Ray. Though terrifying images fled at the sight of her, Josh felt relief weaken his legs as he barreled up the stairs. Wordlessly he stopped beside her. For a long moment, he stared at her, memorizing the sight of her, needing to assure himself that she was free of bruises.

Unsteady and uncertain, Allie realized how much she longed for his embrace. "What a night," she said in a weak voice.

He heard the tremble in her voice. "Easy," he soothed. Whether she wanted his embrace or not no longer mattered. Even if she would accept nothing else from him, he needed to offer her comfort. He prepared himself, expecting her to pull away as he curled an arm around her shoulder and drew her to him.

She leaned into him, releasing a hard breath. As his eyes floated over her with a caress as gentle and yet as sturdy as his touch, she felt him binding her to him. "I thought that I heard someone in the building."

Josh glanced at the officer still standing at the bottom of the steps. "And you called the police?"

Allie anticipated his anger. "No. I decided that I was acting jumpy, so I went into the hallway. I saw Chad's shadow. At least, I was certain it was his."

His hand tightened measurably on her shoulder. "Was it?"

"Yes." Beneath the hand on his chest, Allie felt his heart pounding as if it would burst through. She rushed words to soften his fury. "He was headed toward the broadcasting booth, so I hurried to the office to reach a phone. When I got there, I—" Her voice trailed off in response to footsteps behind them.

"I'm sorry," Neil said in passing. He kept walking, urged forward by the officer's grip on his arm. "You understand, don't you, Allie?" he asked, looking back.

Sadness washed over her as she nodded. For a long moment, she stared after him, following his movements down the stairs until the police ushered him out the door.

Josh swung a puzzled look at Ray. "Neil?"

At the knot lodged in her throat, Allie swallowed hard before answering, "Yes, Neil. I caught him sneaking out of my office. Inside it was another threatening note."

"Why?" he asked angrily. "Why would he do that to you? You were his friend."

"All he ever talked about was success," she said with a semblance of understanding. "He said that he needed me to go to Los Angeles with him. He was beginning to worry that I wouldn't take the job. He thought I was falling in love with you," she said softly. "So he tried to frighten me, make me believe that someone was after me." She raised her chin a fraction. "It's obvious that he believed he could convince me to run. If I felt threatened, he assumed that I'd be eager to leave."

"But," Ray cut in, "he made one final threat and got caught."

Allie grinned wryly. "Thanks to Chad."

"What has Chad got to do with this?" Josh asked with a hint of annoyance because of his own confusion.

"The police questioned him, too," Ray said. "It seems Chad had come back to the radio station. He'd set the emergency exit lock before he'd left earlier. He wanted to get back in to talk to Allie alone. But he didn't find her in the broadcasting booth," Ray went on. "When he walked down the hall, he saw Neil sneaking around. Chad rushed into my office and called the police then."

Looking up, she saw Chad descending the stairs and released her death grip on Josh's arm.

As Josh whipped around, too, Chad shrunk back as if he expected Josh to unleash anger for another man on him.

Allie waited until Chad reached the bottom step then grabbed his hand. "Thank you."

He returned a sheepish grin. "I didn't know what to do," he admitted. "I only came to talk to you. But I could tell that he was up to no good. There had been talk around the radio station about you receiving threatening letters. I—I didn't know if he was the one or not."

Allie squeezed his hand firmly. "I thought you were the one."

His eyes widened. "Me?"

She paused and laughed softly at herself, "I thought you were following me at the radio station."

His face twisted into a grimace. "Sort of," he admitted in a hesitant manner, glancing at Josh again. "Only around the radio station though," he said quickly. "I want to learn broadcasting." An embarrassed flush swept over his face. "I admire you a lot. I wanted to learn how to be one of the best," he added with some hesitation.

Her own reflection had never been clear to her, she realized.

"I thought if I listened to you, I'd learn. I like your program. You don't cut everything and everyone apart like the other deejays. People call, and you listen. You make them feel that they're not alone. I'd like to be able to do that."

"Then, we'll have to talk, won't we?"

He beamed. "Tomorrow?"

She placed her other hand over his. "I'll see you tomorrow."

Sticking his hands in his pockets, Josh waited only until Chad was out of earshot. "He has a crush on you," he said with certainty.

"He's nearly ten years younger than me, Josh."

"And he's got a crush on you."

Ray laughed easily. "He's right, Allie. I'm afraid that you're going to have to deal with him now."

Allie returned his smile. "I'm not concerned."

Too many emotions plagued Josh for jealousy to take root.

"I guess that I don't have to worry about you any more, Allie," Ray quipped with a smiling glance at Josh while they strolled down the stairs.

Josh wished that he could say the same. No matter where Allie was, he would think about her and worry about her.

Ray reached forward to open the exit door. "I can't tell you how many times I wanted to stop, Allie, and talk about Neil. But—" He paused, shaking his head and waiting until they stood outside. "As the station's general manager, I didn't have a right to interfere in personal business. And the offer that Neil brought to you was just that until you turned in your resignation."

Her brows bunched with her frown. "You know, I realized how much Neil wanted fame, but I'm still puzzled. The Los Angeles station was offering us the morning show. But there was open airtime for a single deejay. He could have gone with that even if I had told him no."

Ray shook his head emphatically. "No, he couldn't. That's what he thought you'd believe. It was never true." An expression of disgust flitted across his face. "Don't feel too sorry for him. He's not the person that you think he is. After Neil learned that someone would be asked to take over for Junior, he came to me," Ray explained as they started walking toward their cars. "Neil wanted the program director's position. He kept prodding me for an answer. He learned that you were our first choice.

"But my problems began *before* you announced that a new program director would be hired."

"That's why I feel responsible. Neil knew before anyone else did. He'd overheard Bill Vannen and me talking. I couldn't deny that a change was going to be made. That's when he said that he wanted it and learned about you. A few days later," Ray said, rubbing a hand across his unshaven jaw, "I heard the talk about the Los Angeles deal. Neil had called them."

Puzzlement edged her voice. "He said that they called him."

"Another lie. I suppose that's when he became desperate."

"Why?"

"Because the general manager in Los Angeles is a friend of mine. He called me. He told me that the California offer wasn't really for Neil. They wanted you. Neil had to guarantee you or there was no deal. I told my friend that we were offering you the program director's position here. We laughed about it. You know, may the best man win kind of conversation. I never realized how desperate Neil was feeling at that point. He was riding on your shirttail, Allie. Your success."

Mentally she laughed as his words registered in her mind. *Her* success.

"And we're thrilled that we've got you," Ray said on a gruff laugh.

Josh stilled abruptly and grabbed her arm to stop her. "You're staying?"

"Yes, I'm staying," she said softly, facing him. "I told Ray minutes ago that I wanted the program director's job."

Ray sent them both a knowing expression. "It seems this was a night of surprises." On a wink, he stepped away. "I'll get someone to fill in for you tonight, Allie. Enjoy a day off," he called back, not bothering to look at them.

Achingly Josh wanted to take her in his arms, but he couldn't force her to accept him or love him. And he couldn't go back to the way things had been. He would want it all with her, including marriage and children. He'd found the job he'd always wanted with a security built on decades of existence. He'd met people whom he would finally have time to call friends. He'd met a woman who brought the laughter and fun that he'd known as a child back into his life. But love wasn't simple for him. Too much from his past still lingered. He needed the kind of love that was rock-solid and so firmly rooted with certainties that no changing winds could sway it.

Serious eyes, Allie thought, not for the first time. He had such serious eyes.

"What changed your mind about leaving?"

"Several things. I'd convinced myself that I wanted to leave. But I was fooling myself—running. I thought that I could escape all the demands that my family seemed trapped by. But after my mother called, I realized that I wasn't any different. I thought that I was free because I never allowed myself to be tied down to something or someone like everyone in the family had. I wanted to be free of demands from other people."

She shook her head. "Josh, I've worried for so long. I worried about leading a life like everyone in my family," she said, desperately trying to make him understand. "I didn't want my work to overshadow everything else. I didn't want to struggle my life away trying to be a success in a profession that eventually would trap me. And I hadn't wanted a marriage similar to theirs."

A need to reassure her tightened like a hard ball in his stomach.

"But I haven't been any more free than a sister who's chained to a job that she doesn't like or a sister who's bound to a husband she wants to divorce. They placed demands on themselves. So did I. I kept placing a demand on myself not to be satisfied anywhere."

As she looked away, he followed her gaze toward the sunrise. Had he fallen in love with her on that day weeks ago when they shared special moments with each other or during that first moment that he'd seen her? A weariness weakened him. He fought himself to keep from pulling her in his arms. She was staying, but was he a part of her plans? "So you'll stay." He shoved his hands in his pockets. "For a while? Forever? How long?"

She saw no smile in his eyes and felt muscles tense at the back of her neck. Bravery came in many forms, Allie realized. She felt a cowardly streak grabbing hold as she realized that she had to make the first move this time. She frowned with apprehension, unsure, not of what she should do, but how to go about it. "I hurt you, yet you came here."

He'd overcome dozens of disappointments and failures in his life, sometimes by setting pride aside. For her, for the one thing he wanted more than anything else in his life, he could brush it away again. When she shivered, he opened his arms to her. "Come here. You look like you need some warming."

"A lot," she answered softly.

"Allie, Barrington is everything I thought that I was missing from my life." He stroked her arm lightly. "I can make a home here, have friends, have a sense of belonging. Or I thought that I could until I met you. Now, I'm not certain any of it would matter if you're not here, too," he admitted.

Hearing a noticeable roughness in his voice, she caressed his cheek as she fought tears. He was telling her that nothing mattered but her. Few people had ever offered such unselfish love to her before. What manner of man had she nearly let slip away, who could love so strongly that he didn't know how to give up? she wondered. "I don't know why I was leaving Barrington. Or you. I didn't feel something better could be found in California. But then, I've been running away my whole life," she managed in a quiet voice. She trembled with emotion. "I don't have to go anywhere else any more. This is where I want to be."

As he saw the sparkle in her eyes, uncertainty melted away.

"I'm a success at the one thing, the most important thing in life. And so are you." She leaned closer. "It's something they've all failed at. I know how to love someone else." The wind tossed her hair forward and blew at her back as if nudging her against him. "I do love you," she said softly.

He plunged his hands in her hair to hold her face still. "Oh, God, I've been waiting for those words," he said brokenly. He hadn't believed that he could love her more than he had before, but he needed it all with her. Nothing less would do. "Do you love me enough to marry me?"

No hesitation burdened her. She inched even closer and slid her arms around his back. "I planned to ask you if necessary." He closed his mouth over hers with a fierceness that rocked her. Long and deep, the kiss bound them to each other, and she trembled as love and joy mingled together.

"No doubts?" he murmured against her lips.

"None," she said in a tone filled with firm conviction and happiness. "I've always thought that you were perfect for me."

On a laugh, he urged her toward his car. As she swayed close, brushing her hip against his, he tightened his grip on her waist. "Funny, that was my thought exactly."

Reaching the car, Allie turned into his arms to face him. A trace of seriousness flashed in to her eyes. "No one is perfect but some people are perfect for each other, aren't they?"

"Some people are," he whispered against her mouth, taking another quick taste.

Chapter Thirteen

"Which direction should we go?" Allie asked as they climbed the stairs toward their apartments.

"Mine. I'll make you dinner."

"Breakfast," she said on a laugh, dropping her head to his shoulder. "I'm going on your timetable, Professor. We'll have mornings together before work."

"And nights." As she raised her face to his, he arched a brow that drew her giggle.

Allie pressed her lips to his cheek. "And nights," she repeated softly. She pulled back with the sound of her ringing telephone. On a sigh, she released his hand. "I'll meet you. Five minutes," she said, walking backwards and holding her fingers up. "No more."

"More than five and we'll forget breakfast."

Allie laughed at his feigned threatening look and rushed into her apartment. The last person she expected a call from was her mother. While they went through their quick greeting, Allie decided now was as good a time as any to relate her good news. "I'm surprised to hear from you so soon."

"Soon?"

"We just talked," Allie reminded her. "Why are you calling again? Is there some new crisis with Marilyn?"

"She and Roger have agreed that it's in their best interest to offer the right image."

Allie wasn't surprised.

"Did Marilyn ever call you back?"

"No."

"I was sure that she'd call and tell you. Do you realize how many times she looked to you for help when things were unpleasant in her life?"

Caught off-balance by her words, Allie took a moment to battle confusion. "She never asked me for advice."

"Of course, she did."

"Mother, she didn't."

"Allison, I happen to know that she called you constantly whenever she had a problem."

"She has never called except to tell me what I should do or shouldn't do. Or to remind me that—"

Her mother's soft laugh stopped her. "She called you during troubled times. Whether you realize it or not, she probably asked you more questions regarding her problems than your own. She's a lawyer. An excellent one," her mother reminded her. "She's wonderful at getting answers from people without them knowing that they're giving them."

Something similar to shock rippled through her. Allie leaned back and closed her eyes for a second, trying to recall the previous conversations with her sister. Repeatedly Marilyn had asked questions regarding marriage. Stupidly Allie had assumed her sister was nagging her to get married. "And so she and Roger will both be unhappy all for the sake of success."

Her mother spoke softly. "You've never understood that they weren't like you. You always knew what you wanted. You've always been satisfied with your life."

"Satisfied?" Allie murmured. In her whole life, she doubted that anything she ever heard again would dumbfound her in the same way. She'd never been satisfied. Didn't they realize that? Of course, they didn't. A tiny sense of loss constricted her throat, for they didn't seem to know her any better than she knew them.

"I also called to tell you—" Her mother paused as if the words were caught in her throat. "Your father is getting married again."

Allie heard a strain in her mother's voice and stilled. Feelings she'd never expected suddenly overwhelmed her. Her mother had loved her father, Allie realized in that instant, and no one had known. She'd never allowed anyone to know. Why hadn't she? With something near despair, Allie wished she could hug her, offer her a second of affection, yet she couldn't. Distance of not only miles but also years separated them. But some sense of what her mother had done reached her. Protectively she'd tried to shield her daughters from the same pain. She'd urged marriages built on something more predictable than love, not because love eluded a Gentry, but because she feared they would experience the heartbreak of it. Someone had to take the first of many steps, Allie realized. "Mother, I'm sorry."

"S-sorry?"

"This must be very difficult for you," Allie said, determined not to let this chance for closeness with her slip away. "Mother?"

"We've been divorced many—"

Allie cut in. "Still, some feelings make it difficult."

Reluctantly she conceded, "Yes. Yes, it is."

Allie swallowed hard. She heard the sadness for something that had been longed for and had been lost.

"Thank you for understanding," her mother said in a firmer tone.

"I finally do," Allie admitted softly.

"But she's—" her mother managed. "Well, she's young. Twenty-nine, I believe. Young enough to trudge through the jungles with him."

Allie slouched on the sofa cushion and twisted the telephone cord around her finger. "And they'll no doubt send one of us a fertility mask."

Her mother offered a soft genuine laugh. "No doubt. And who'll want it?"

"Me. Something has happened here since I talked to you last."

"Oh?"

"I have a new job."

"Are you becoming forgetful? You told me you were moving to California," she said in a tone laced with faint criticism.

Some things will never change, Allie reminded herself. "No, I'm staying here. I'm going to be the program director at the same radio station. They want me to make the station number one."

"And you want to stay? You want to do that for a while?" she asked in a surprised tone.

Allie heard Josh's footsteps in the hall. "Oh, I'm sure it will be for a long time." Allie yawned, suddenly aware it was her usual bedtime. Too much excitement, she mused. Too much happiness. Tired or not, she'd never sleep. "I'm getting married."

"Married!"

Allie ticked off several seconds before her mother finally responded. "You told us that you'd never get married."

"People change."

"Is he—is he another one of those rock stars?"

Of course, she would expect him to be a little wild, a little unconventional, an opposite of what she should have chosen. Allie imagined that she was holding her breath, praying her new son-in-law wouldn't go to the wedding decked out in leather and chains, a multicolored punk haircut and earrings that dangled to his shoulders. "No. He's not a musician."

"Allison I don't—"

"He owns a suit, Mother."

At Allie's laugh, her mother sighed.

"He's a professor of history."

The phone was dead for a full minute.

"Are you there?" Allie asked.

"I'm here," her mother returned. "A professor?"

As Josh strolled in, Allie released a long, relieved sigh. She stretched out, plopping her feet on the carton before her while she eyed the bucket that he'd carried in. "Yes."

Setting down the bucket, he mouthed, who?

She clamped her hand over the receiver. "My mother." Rubbernecking, she frowned that she couldn't see what the bucket contained. "You'll like him," she said into the receiver.

Josh made a comical face and lowered himself to the sofa beside her.

"He's very proper," she added and winked at him before curling closer. "Yes," Allie managed softly as his knuckles brushed her jaw. "I remembered the party you're having. Yes, we'll come." She reached across him and set the receiver in its cradle.

With a fingertip beneath her chin, he turned her face back to his. "What did your mother want?"

"She called to tell me that my father is about to give matrimony a second try," she said, stretching forward again to look around him. "What's in the bucket?"

"And what did she think of all of your news?"

"She wants to meet you."

Josh grinned wryly in answer. He would reserve his judgment of her family until after he'd met them. "I'm looking forward to it."

"You're a glutton for punishment, aren't you?"

"I want to thank them. For you," he whispered against her mouth.

Lightly she nipped at his bottom lip.

"One request." He tightened his embrace, and leading with his shoulder, he rolled her with him to the carpeting.

Snug beneath him, she laughed, a husky laugh, while she skimmed his back and hip. "Only one?"

"Only one," he said while dipping a hand into the bucket.

Curious, she pushed her head back and raised her eyes to see behind her. "What do you have in—" Laughter cut her words short as leaves fell around her. "You're crazy."

"I'm learning."

Smilingly she coiled her arms around his back and dragged him close to her. In his eyes, she saw the love that she'd always longed for. "What's your one request?"

"Never change your mind."

"Never," she murmured before his lips captured hers.

* * * * *

Silhouette Books®

PASSPORT TO ROMANCE VACATION SWEEPSTAKES

OFFICIAL RULES

SWEEPSTAKES RULES AND REGULATIONS. NO PURCHASE NECESSARY.

HOW TO ENTER:

1. To enter, complete this official entry form and return with your invoice in the envelope provided, or print your name, address, telephone number and age on a plain piece of paper and mail to: Passport to Romance, P.O. Box #1397, Buffalo, N.Y. 14269-1397. No mechanically reproduced entries accepted.
2. All entries must be received by the Contest Closing Date, midnight, December 31, 1990 to be eligible.
3. Prizes: There will be ten (10) Grand Prizes awarded, each consisting of a choice of a trip for two people to: i) London, England (approximate retail value $5,050 U.S.); ii) England, Wales and Scotland (approximate retail value $6,400 U.S.); iii) Caribbean Cruise (approximate retail value $7,300 U.S.); iv) Hawaii (approximate retail value $ 9,550 U.S.); v) Greek Island Cruise in the Mediterranean (approximate retail value $12,250 U.S.); vi) France (approximate retail value $7,300 U.S.).
4. Any winner may choose to receive any trip or a cash alternative prize of $5,000.00 U.S. in lieu of the trip.
5. Odds of winning depend on number of entries received.
6. A random draw will be made by Nielsen Promotion Services, an independent judging organization on January 29, 1991, in Buffalo, N.Y., at 11:30 a.m. from all eligible entries received on or before the Contest Closing Date. Any Canadian entrants who are selected must correctly answer a time-limited, mathematical skill-testing question in order to win. Quebec residents may submit any litigation respecting the conduct and awarding of a prize in this contest to the Régie des loteries et courses du Quebec.
7. Full contest rules may be obtained by sending a stamped, self-addressed envelope to: "Passport to Romance Rules Request", P.O. Box 9998, Saint John, New Brunswick, E2L 4N4.
8. Payment of taxes other than air and hotel taxes is the sole responsibility of the winner.
9. Void where prohibited by law.

PASSPORT TO ROMANCE VACATION SWEEPSTAKES

OFFICIAL RULES

SWEEPSTAKES RULES AND REGULATIONS. NO PURCHASE NECESSARY.

HOW TO ENTER:

1. To enter, complete this official entry form and return with your invoice in the envelope provided, or print your name, address, telephone number and age on a plain piece of paper and mail to: Passport to Romance, P.O. Box #1397, Buffalo, N.Y. 14269-1397. No mechanically reproduced entries accepted.
2. All entries must be received by the Contest Closing Date, midnight, December 31, 1990 to be eligible.
3. Prizes: There will be ten (10) Grand Prizes awarded, each consisting of a choice of a trip for two people to: i) London, England (approximate retail value $5,050 U.S.); ii) England, Wales and Scotland (approximate retail value $6,400 U.S.); iii) Caribbean Cruise (approximate retail value $7,300 U.S.); iv) Hawaii (approximate retail value $ 9,550 U.S.); v) Greek Island Cruise in the Mediterranean (approximate retail value $12,250 U.S.); vi) France (approximate retail value $7,300 U.S.).
4. Any winner may choose to receive any trip or a cash alternative prize of $5,000.00 U.S. in lieu of the trip.
5. Odds of winning depend on number of entries received.
6. A random draw will be made by Nielsen Promotion Services, an independent judging organization on January 29, 1991, in Buffalo, N.Y., at 11:30 a.m. from all eligible entries received on or before the Contest Closing Date. Any Canadian entrants who are selected must correctly answer a time-limited, mathematical skill-testing question in order to win. Quebec residents may submit any litigation respecting the conduct and awarding of a prize in this contest to the Régie des loteries et courses du Quebec.
7. Full contest rules may be obtained by sending a stamped, self-addressed envelope to· "Passport to Romance Rules Request", P.O. Box 9998, Saint John, New Brunswick, E2L 4N4.
8. Payment of taxes other than air and hotel taxes is the sole responsibility of the winner
9. Void where prohibited by law.

 RLS-DIR

VACATION SWEEPSTAKES

MONTH 1 ENTRY

Official Entry Form

Yes, enter me in the drawing for one of ten Vacations-for-Two! If I'm a winner, I'll get my choice of any of the six different destinations being offered — and I won't have to decide until after I'm notified!

Return entries with invoice in envelope provided along with Daily Travel Allowance Voucher. Each book in your shipment has two entry forms — and the more you enter, the better your chance of winning!

Name

Address Apt.

City State/Prov. Zip/Postal Code

Daytime phone number ____________
Area Code

☐ I am enclosing a Daily Travel Allowance Voucher in the amount of $__________ Write in amount revealed beneath scratch-off

PASSPORT
WIN
1 of 10 Vacations
SEE INSIDE
TO ROMANCE

VACATION SWEEPSTAKES

MONTH 1 ENTRY

Official Entry Form

Yes, enter me in the drawing for one of ten Vacations-for-Two! If I'm a winner, I'll get my choice of any of the six different destinations being offered — and I won't have to decide until after I'm notified!

Return entries with invoice in envelope provided along with Daily Travel Allowance Voucher. Each book in your shipment has two entry forms — and the more you enter, the better your chance of winning!

Name

Address Apt.

City State/Prov. Zip/Postal Code

Daytime phone number ____________
Area Code

☐ I am enclosing a Daily Travel Allowance Voucher in the amount of $__________ Write in amount revealed beneath scratch-off

CPS-ONE